Tainted Evidence

A Lieutenant Beaudry novel

Michael Kent

MEZZO PUBLICATIONS

Montreal Canada

ISBN-13: 978-1-7751642-7-2 print book
ISBN-13: 978-1-7751642-8-9 electronic book

Cover art Design by RLSather/Peherte Design

THIS ONE IS DEDICATED
TO YOU

To the loyal fans of the Beaudry series, and to mystery
novel readers everywhere.

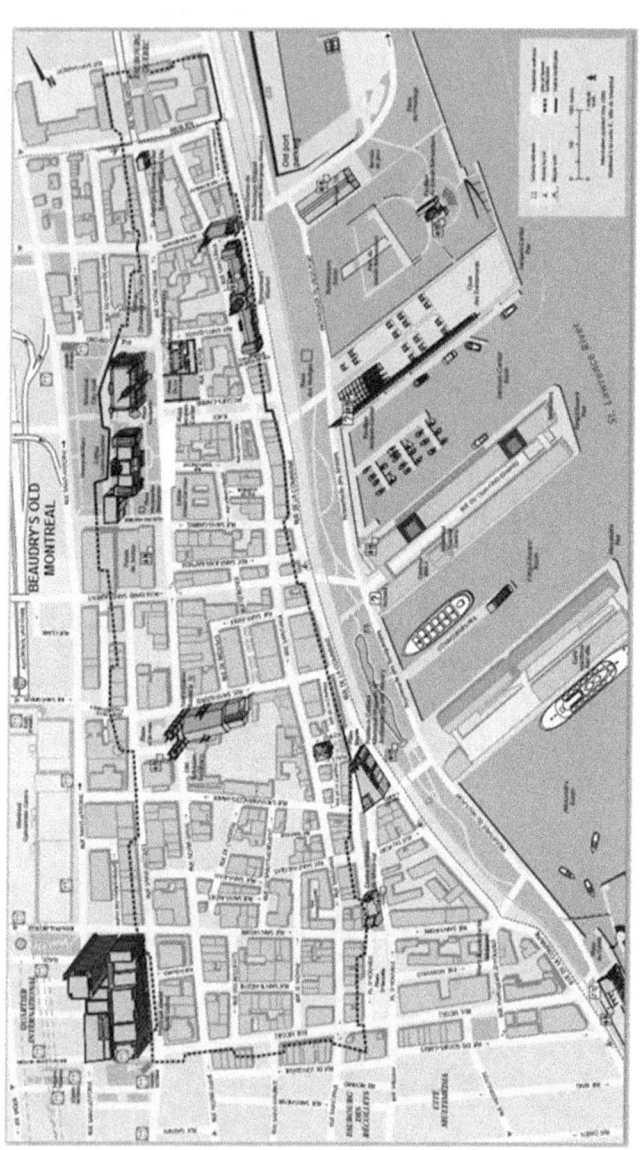

ACKNOWLEDGMENTS

My indebted appreciation, to Don Chambers, Randall Krzak, Sideman, Rachel Parsons, Seabrass and all of the reviewers on The Next Big Writer for their insights, suggestions, and continued support.

A grateful thanks to my editors past and present: Sigrid Macdonald, and Stevie Mikayne whose skillful work keeps Beaudry's adventures correctly punctuated and more concise.

"Facts are stubborn things; and whatever may be our wishes, our inclinations, or the dictates of our passions, they cannot alter the state of facts and evidence."

— **John Adams**

PREFACE

When you are on the Interpol global watch list, air travel is difficult—extremely difficult. But not impossible.

The two hundred and twenty-one passengers from Air France flight 344 crowded into the newly renovated Immigration and Customs hall at Trudeau International Airport. People shuffled single file into the maze of aluminum posts and black ribbon, the start of a slow trek to the passport scanning machines and the glass-sided immigration booths. They talked in low tones as if in a church, everybody tired and anxious to get home, or to whatever business had brought them to Montreal on this warm, muggy, August day.

Forty-third in line, Maître Paul Laverdière—or so his passport claimed him to be, ran nervous fingers along the handle of his battered leather briefcase, as if fondling prayer beads. The wait to pass customs and immigration always unleashed butterflies in his stomach. He ignored the queasy feeling by telling himself his cover story and his papers were impeccable.

He quite well resembled the picture in his French passport. Clean shaven, hairstyle parted down the center and tinted Clairol medium hazelnut.

His dress style was what one would expect of a French notary: scuffed brown oxfords, blue serge suit over an off-white shirt complemented by a sober grey and black polka-dot bow tie. He *was* Maître Laverdière.

For the sixth time in as many minutes, he ran the back of his left hand upwards against his cheek. The delays in the departure from Paris had added hours to his travel time. His strong beard was growing fast, and could soon betray his careful disguise.

He muttered under his breath, "Let's go, let's go," as though to make the line move faster.

As if his impatience had jinxed it, all forward progress stopped, and amid comments and whispers from up front, people started laying their carry-on cases on the floor.

Shifting his weight from one foot to the other, he edged sideways to see what caused the commotion.

Ahead, two children giggled as a customs officer and a handler led a frisky beagle down the queue towards him.

The little brown dog had a circle of white fur on his left side, and a smaller one on his forehead. The animal swiveled his head rapidly from side to side as if he were a flashlight scanning the dark. He pranced down the line, sniffing at handbags and cases, his tail wagging merrily, until he reached the passenger fifth in front of Laverdière. The dog suddenly sat down, emitting a throaty *ooof*, like an old man dropping his overweight rear into a Barcalounger.

The passengers moved back from the young man as if he were contaminated.

The beagle's target asked the handler, "Why is he staring at me? I didn't do anything." Laverdière caught a glimpse of a reddening face under long dirty-blond hair. He quickly sidestepped back in line, trying to blend into the few people in front of him.

A few minutes later, Laverdière presented his documents at the immigration booth. The scan showed the passport to be authentic.

The man led off by police was a disguised blessing, catching everyone's attention.

Even the unsmiling immigration officer looked over Laverdière's shoulder to watch the dog's quarry led away. His interest elsewhere, he barely glanced at the man in front of him as he stamped the document for entry.

"How long will you be in Canada, Monsieur Laverdière?"

"Ah, my business should take about a week." He replied in perfect French.

Traveling with only a briefcase and an overnight bag, Maître Laverdière rushed towards the exit and flagged the first taxi in the line.

He slammed the cab door and made a forward brushing motion to the driver. "The Queen Elisabeth Hotel."

He sat in the car, buoyant with relief. Allah was indeed merciful. If his luck held, it would take weeks before anyone found the body of the real Notaire Laverdière. By then, it would be too late—he'd have finished the contract. If all went according to plan, four more eliminations, added to the thirty-two accomplished over the last five years, would significantly add to his bank account, and as well, assure his reputation as the best *accidental death* assassin in the world.

- 1 -

Predictions were for one of the warmest days this summer. At 8:10, the temperature was already 26°C. I had finished my morning swim and was enjoying breakfast on the restaurant patio when the waiter stopped at my table.

"I see you're doing justice to our blueberry pancakes, Lieutenant. Would you like more coffee?"

"Lieutenant? Where did you get that from?"

"You were on the late news yesterday. Something about you beating up four guys in a bar fight."

"It was a poolroom. I had an arrest warrant for a guy, and some of his biker friends decided to interfere."

"The news said four against one. I saw you do some fancy martial arts stuff on the beach this morning. Is that what saved you?"

"My Tai-chi is for flexibility and relaxation. What saved me was clean living and the three ball. Surprising how docile people get when cracked on the head with a Brunswick Centennial."

Before I could regale him with a blow-by-blow chronicle of the pool hall fight, my Irish redhead significant other walked up behind him. She sat next to me on the same bench and ordered a smidgen of fruit and a cup of green tea. The waiter left as I kissed her cheek.

"Is that all you're having for breakfast?"

"I have to maintain my shape." Pat said, as she fluffed her hair at me.

"I'm pretty sure I perused every inch of your shape last night. I didn't find any parts that I didn't like. In fact, a few areas were exquisite."

"Perusing, is that what you call it? Methinks it's just himself boasting because I let you have your way with me."

"I'm not sure who seduced whom. I suppose you just accidently packed the near-transparent teddy for our vacation."

"It's light and cool. I was quite warm last evening. You plied me with wine," Pat said with a lascivious grin.

After more than a year together, I was still in awe of her. That such a beautiful and smart woman would fall for a big over-muscled cop like me was a mystery.

My cell phone, in vibe mode, rattled against my empty orange juice glass. During our repartee, my right hand, with a will of its own, had drifted up Pat's leg. She rapped my fingers with the back of her spoon. "Answer your phone, ya big gombeen."

The screen identified the caller as my boss, Pat's uncle, homicide Captain Jean O'Neil.

I answered, "Lieutenant Beaudry's on vacation, leave a message—beep."

"Very funny Robert. I'm calling you as a favor, so you wouldn't learn it from the news."

"Learn what?"

"Aldo DiLalla, your friend Nico's cousin, was murdered last night."

"I can be back in Montreal in a couple of hours," I said.

Pat gave me a look that, notwithstanding today's heat and humidity, put frost on my coffee.

"Absolutely not, you're still on Internal Affair's follow-up list for last week's fight," Jean said. "I don't want you near this investigation. You're too close to the people involved. The family called Nico direct. In his zeal to help, he contaminated the crime scene and made a mess of everything. He tainted a lot of evidence and wound up suspended.

Probably due to hanging around you too often. You taught him well."

In my mind's eye, I could envision the captain leaning back in his ratty green leather desk chair, both sides of his little gray caterpillar mustache turned down, his usual snarky look when addressing me.

"Thanks for the compliment boss, and thanks for calling me. I'll be back in the office on Monday."

"Don't mention it," was the last thing I heard before the line went dead.

"What was that about? Uncle called to compliment you?"

"Not exactly. Nico's cousin got whacked. The family called him direct instead of nine-one-one. He rushed over, made a mess of the crime scene, and got suspended."

"I'm gobsmacked that Nico acted the fool. That's not his style."

"Aldo was his favorite cousin. When family is involved—." I gave Pat the Italian wrist-turning, open-palm, hand sign for, 'who knows?'

Pat sighed and up-raised her eyes. "We're booked for two more days of vacation, but you best call Nico. He may need you."

I'd been friends with Detective Sergeant Nico DiLalla since our academy days. Added to his kindness in adopting me as part of his large Italian family, he was a good, honest cop, not an easy path to maintain when you're in the narcotics squad.

The fact that some of his family were reputed to be on the other side of the badge didn't help his chances of advancement in the department. His name was on Internal Affairs list of favorite cops to harass. Probably a few slots down from mine.

I speed-dialed Nico. The call went direct to voice mail. A few minutes later, I dialed again with the same result. I tried his home. His wife answered on the second ring.

"Carmen, *mi dispiache*, I just heard about Aldo. How's Nico?"

"I've never seen him so upset. He's a walking vendetta with no target. He's at the funeral home taking care of the arrangements for the family."

"I called him. All I got was voice mail."

"Internal Affairs took his phone. He's using mine."

I told Carmen that I would check on Nico and help where I could. It didn't seem to comfort her much. My bad-boy reputation didn't allay her unspoken fears that Nico might be treading on dangerous grounds.

I got Nico after the fifth ring.

"I was about to hang up," I said.

"Not used to this phone," Nico said. "You heard?"

"My captain called me. I'm up North at a spa with Pat. I was told by the I.A. pencil pushers to get lost for a week while they finished the paperwork on my arrest of Brody and the incidental victims of the poolroom fight. What's the story on your cousin?"

"Shot, while in his car, in his own driveway."

"I heard you got into a bit of trouble at the scene," I said.

"Now I know why you joke about your I.A. nemesis Trehearne. He's a real *coglione*. He had me suspended for tampering with evidence, minutes after he stepped on a shell casing next to the car. *Fortunato* I have another in my jacket."

"What are you doing with evidence in your pocket?" I asked as calmly as I could.

"A black dude showed up with the I.A. guys, a big guy, weightlifter type, not as large as you, but close. Said he was in charge of the case. I don't know him, and I don't trust him to find Aldo's killers. I was saving pieces of evidence for you."

"Thanks for your confidence but my boss doesn't want me near that case," I said, "But... hang on to your illicit evidence. I'll find out what I can from my sources, and we'll meet for supper when I get back to town Sunday evening. *Va bene*?"

Before we hung up, we set the meeting at a French bistro close to my downtown apartment.

Pat spread her hands palms up. "It's beyond me how you can be on vacation, far removed from a case, and still manage to tear out a couple of pages from the procedure manual."

"It's an inborn talent," I said, as I laid my hand gently on her knee.

- 2 -

The last two days of our mini-vacation flashed by like an F-18 on a missed carrier landing.

After our hedonistic week at the fancy health spa in the Laurentian Mountains North of Montreal, we headed back to reality, and Pat's house. We were a couple, but still lived apart. My downtown bachelor pad was too small for both of us, and the large and unruly Maine Coon that had adopted me a year ago. Her west-suburbs divorce-settlement house was too far from my east-end Major Crimes head office.

For now, commuting from house to house seemed to work—*if it's not broke, don't fix it* applied to our situation.

"Call me when you finish your supper with Nico," Pat said. "I want to find out what happened. And don't plan any shenanigans that'll get you in trouble now."

"Woman of little faith. I have no intention of antagonizing the Tweedledee and Tweedledumb team from *Infernal* affairs anymore than I already have. At least not this week."

"Well that puts my mind at ease, doesn't it now?"

I gave Pat a silly grin. "Are you sleeping over at my place later?"

"I'm still trying to catch my breath from last night, and I have an early meeting with a crown prosecutor. I'll pass on your kind offer."

"Aww, Crackers will miss purring on your lap."

Pat ignored my comment and pointed ahead.

"Holy saints in heaven, what happened to Montreal?"

In the distance, we saw the city skyline. A dome of dirty brown fog covered the island.

"Must be some type of temperature inversion," I said. "For once, the weather guessers got it right. This afternoon is hotter than a devil's fart. All the moisture and pollution is trapped under a layer of warmer air."

"Crude, but appropriate simile," Pat said with a scowl. "We come back from a week of fresh air and exercise to breathe this poison. Just lovely."

"I deduce a hint of upset in your tone," I said.

"I'm not looking forward to getting back to the job. I joined the anti-corruption squad to catch the crooked politicians and contractors that have been stealing millions of our tax dollars." Pat looked down and shook her head, red curls hiding her eyes.

"Now I'm stuck in court most of my week listening to slimy lawyers finagle deals to get the gurriers off with token fines and light slaps on the wrist."

"You do the best job you can. We have a good legal system. It doesn't always mean it's a good justice system," I said.

Pat leaned her head on my shoulder and we drove in silence, each of us in our own thought bubble.

In retrospect, I should have questioned her more about her worries.

* * *

I had dropped Pat off at her house and picked up Crackers from my neighbor. It was the first time Paul had taken care of my crazy cat for more than a day. I was certain it would be the last, his misdeeds unforgiven, even after I paid for the decapitated Angel Wing Begonia and the shattered vase.

With the exception of the tip end of his black fluffy tail, Crackers, in full feline moping-mood was hidden under my living room sofa. I now had a girlfriend that had declined my bed, and a cat that would pout and ignore me for a few days as my punishment for having left him for a week.

I needed to hunt for information on the death of Nico's cousin; I hoped I'd have better luck with my police contacts and street informants. I poured myself a small tumbler of Glenfiddich single malt and sat at the kitchen table with my notebook, my phone at the ready, and many unanswered questions.

- 3 -

My sixteen-minute fast-walk to the bistro was good for the legs and circulation, but with today's pollution, it was probably a negative health benefit on the lungs. The air had a foul tang, like the sweat of a guilty man.

Luc, the owner, came out of the kitchen and steered me to my usual booth. He took the little black-and-gold printed 'Reserved' sign off the table and placed it on the next one.

"I didn't call ahead," I said. "If you have it held for someone else, another table is okay."

"Tradition has this as your table, *Monsieur* Lieutenant. Are you dining with your lady this evening?"

"No, she skipped this Sunday." I slipped into the booth.

"Ah," Luc ran his finger down his long crooked nose, his nervous tell before asking an indiscreet question. "I hope not a love problem. Over the years, I have seen you dine here with many lady friends. Some of them may have scratched your heart Robert, but this one, I think can break it, *non*?"

"It shows that much?" I said.

Nico came into the restaurant and strode briskly up to us; it put a period to my question and Luc headed back to his kitchen.

As usual, Nico was dressed as if he had just walked out of a men's fashion magazine shoot for this year's ten most handsome cops and firemen. He sat across from me.

"Isn't it a bit warm for the dress jacket and pocket handkerchief look?"

"Boglioli, from Milano. Linen and silk, light as air, actually, lighter than the air today."

"Yes, the streets stink like a bad alibi," I said. "I'm sure this rare Montreal pollution isn't good for the health. Speaking of unhealthy, you look like you haven't slept in two days."

Nico's usual smile was absent. Above his four o'clock shadow, his face was ashen and his eyes reflected a crimson tint of fatigue.

Before Nico could answer, one of Luc's new and very pretty waitresses brought a basket of bread and spiced olive oil dip to the table. She took one look at Nico; her eyes went magnetic and locked onto his. She ran her tongue over her lips and started toying with her hair as she handed him the menu. Nico read her name tag.

"Kamry, pronounced like the car?"

"Yes, but no relation to a Toyota," she said with a smile that instantly dissipated the gloom from Nico's eyes. "I was named after my mother Katherine and my grandmother Mary."

"Ah, if you had been a car," Nico said with a smile. "You would not be a Toyota, *probabilmente* a curvy Ferrari or Bugatti."

I burst the bubble when I asked what the special of the day was. We went with her recommendation of beef bavette in a blackcurrant jelly sauce, but traded today's French wine suggestion for an upscale bottle of Ripasso Bosan. I had a suspicion that this evening might be a two-bottle supper.

I shook my head. "When our waitress left the table she looked at me as if I had just shot a puppy. You, on the other hand, look like crap today and you still managed to nearly charm the apron off her."

"Roger calls it my *machismo*, and I wouldn't have tried for the apron."

"Where *is* your partner? Was he with you at the scene?"

"No. Rodg's on a two-week sabbatical. He's giving a lecture at an FBI conference in Virginia, something about the criminal mindset."

"Okay, so it's you and me," I said. "Describe the crime scene. Put me in that driveway."

"Aldo was shot while sitting in his car." I could see that Nico's eyes moistening up. "First, I checked if I could revive him, but no. Second, I phoned Uncle Benny. He assured me it had nothing to do with the *family. Non capisco.*"

"I'm not sure that I understand either. I spent hours on the phone trying to get a line on the shooting," I said. "It confirmed what the Don told you. All of my contacts thought it had nothing to do with business. Aldo was a chef, a restaurant owner, not a career criminal. It must have been something personal."

Nico looked down at the table. "Well, he had two restaurants and he was partner in a third, where there might be a money laundering opportunity."

"We're jumping ahead of ourselves," I said. "Let's get back to the scene."

"His car was running, the air turned to full blast, but the driver's window was down. He…shot in the neck, must–must have severed the spinal cord."

"Breathe slowly, Nico. You're not a cop in this, you're the witness. Close your eyes, concentrate, and give me details that stuck with you."

"He had his hands in his lap and his eyes shut. It looked at first as if he was sleeping. No blood at all. Only a half-inch oval dirty pucker on the side of his neck. I had difficulty getting my head around the fact that he was really dead. That's why I tried to revive him." Nico shuddered and opened his eyes.

"You narcotics guys see overdosed addicts every week. A dead person no longer gets to you. But it's not the same when it's close family." I put my hand on his sleeve. "Here comes the wine, let's take a break."

* * *

We had asked Kamry to delay the meal. We nibbled on antipasto, and without remorse, killed the first bottle of wine. In the process, Nico gave me more details of the crime scene. I learned that cousin Aldo had been troubled over something in the week prior to his murder. His wife tearfully told Nico she had berated him for his nightly tossing and turning, and now bitterly regretted her petty complaint. Aldo's difficult and spoiled teen daughter was inconsolable, the close friends incredulous. Who would want to harm such a pillar of the local Italian community?

* * *

By dessert, we were back to business. Nico handed me a Zip-Lock bag containing a small caliber bullet casing. The bottom had the WMR imprint.

"Twenty-two magnum," I said. "An unusual caliber. Not something a pro would normally use."

"Aldo was troubled about something," Nico said. "But not worried about violence. His pocket pistol would have been in his car, not in his safe."

"Gun legally registered?"

Nico took a stab at his cannoli. "Ah—no."

"From what you told me, I'd say the killer was waiting for him. It all happened real fast. Aldo had just got into the car. It must have been boiling inside. He punched the AC to full, opened the window to let out the stale air. The blast of cold on his face made him close his eyes and the fan noise drowned out the sound of someone sneaking up. The dirty looking pucker wound is gunpowder residue. The weapon was at very close range."

Nico took the last bite of cannoli.

"They knew his routine," he said. "Aldo always left for the restaurant at the same time each day."

"They?"

"Vanessa heard the gunshots and rushed out. There was nobody on the street," Nico said. "The killer must have had a getaway car and a driver waiting."

"You haven't told the story to anyone?"

"I'm telling you."

"I'm going to help where I can," I said. "But I can't be officially involved. My boss will suspend me if he finds out I'm meddling. When we spoke yesterday, you said that a big black weightlifter guy was in charge of the case. He isn't black, he's Jamaican brown. Sergeant Manny Agnant, he's a sharp cookie and not with I.A. He's a good cop from the anti-gang squad. I worked with him on a drive-by shooting. My boss probably pulled him in because we're short-staffed due to vacations. Just give him everything you told me."

"You sure?"

"As sure as the bill is on me tonight." I made an air-signing motion to Kamry.

"I'm leaving for Italy end of week," Nico said. "Vanessa said Aldo wished to be buried in the family plot in Cortona."

"In Tuscany?" Are you making a trip of it and bringing your wife and kids?"

"Yes and no," Nico said. "There's a church ceremony at Madonna della Difesa on Wednesday morning. Then Vanessa and I fly the body to Cortona on Thursday, the burial's on Saturday. I have to be back on the job the following Tuesday. We have a big drug raid planned."

"Isn't his sourpuss daughter going with you?" I asked.

"Adrianna never filled out her passport application, and also, she's not speaking to her mother this week. She's going to stay at my house and hang with my two daughters."

"I hope her bratty attitude won't contaminate Sabrina or Marianna."

Nico grimaced and slid his index finger across his throat. "My wife doesn't put up with attitude, not even from me."

"Yeah, Carmen gave me the evil eye more than once," I said. "Adrianna better fly below the radar."

* * *

When I walked Nico back to his car, he insisted on driving me home. As soon as I opened my front door, I heard the sound of Crackers pushing his food bowl around on the kitchen tiles. I opened a can of his favorite fishy mix, as he figure-eight brushed around my legs. While he pawed out scoops onto the floor, his usual "I have to taste it before I eat it" procedure, I called Sergeant Agnant. He answered on the first ring.

"You late, Robert. I'd expected your call yesterday."

"I'll bet the boss told you not to talk to me, nor to give me any information on the Aldo case."

"You win dat bet. But, good friends better dan pocket money. What you want to know?"

Manny validated the information that my contacts had given me. We both agreed it looked like a personal vendetta. He had questioned restaurant employees and suppliers, and so far, found nothing suspicious. Next, he was going to look at business associates, neighbors, and ex-employees. He told me to breathe easy and that he'd call me with progress reports.

I tossed most of my clothes onto the bedroom chair, dropped into bed, and dialed Pat. My intention of suggesting phone sex was fast quelled by the tone of her answer.

"Yes?"

"Am I disturbing something?"

"I was about to fall asleep," she said.

"Sorry, you told me to call you with news from Nico," I said. "You sound pissed off about something. Crackers seems to have forgiven me for abandoning him. Do I have to be forgiven for something I did, or didn't do, on your side?"

"No, no. It's—I got a message that the court trial is delayed, again. I have to drive to Quebec, for three days of more useless meetings, and more political shite."

"My condolences. I'll miss you."

I gave her a summary of my supper conversation with Nico. She kindly expressed confidence that somehow, I would find Aldo's murderer.

After we hung up, I realized I had missed another opportunity to ask Pat what was really bothering her. I've solved homicides in under a week. My cases are solid; I have the best conviction rate in the department. From ten feet away I can read a lie on a criminal's face. I can stare down a thug pointing a .45 at my nose, but understanding women just isn't part of my skill set.

I'd fallen hard for Pat. Maybe my French restaurant-owner friend was right: I could be headed for a big heartbreak.

- 4 -

$\mathbf{Y}$esterday's humid heat had coalesced. The Monday morning sky had dulled to a sad blotchy-gray, the color of a broken promise. The weather guessers were predicting thunderstorms and showers until next Thursday. Not a wonderful start to a new week I thought to myself as I grabbed an umbrella from the closet.

I made it to my Jeep just as the first drops bounced off the asphalt. In mere seconds, the little spikes of rain turned into columns of translucent little soldiers merging to attack the street drain. There are sprinkles, showers, raining cats-and-dogs, and then, there's the magnitude of let's-get-together-

and-build-an-ark. I had rarely seen such a summer downpour. I decided to wait until the mini-monsoon abated before braving the morning traffic and the orange construction cones of Montreal.

I devoted the wait time to case calls.

I dialed Tristan, my contact in the crime lab. His department was FIS, Forensic Identification Section, but since the famed television series, everyone called them the CSI techies.

Before I'd left on vacation, we'd been working on a cold case file. By using a new software program, he had managed to digitize the probable features of a burned-up girl found last year in a shallow grave. His forensics and analytical skills never ceased to impress me. I now had a tool to identify the victim.

My plan to pry information from him on the Aldo case fell apart when someone else answered his phone.

"Tristan Dobson's line, can I help you?"

I recognized the voice of a technician from Dobson's team, a rotund, balding man with Prince Charles ears, but his name escaped me.

"Lieutenant Beaudry, Major Crimes Division. I'd like to speak to Doctor Dobson."

"Oh, my, my, that will be difficult. Tristan is in court testifying as an expert witness all this week. I can give him a message, if you care to leave one."

"It won't be necessary, I have his cell number. Thank you."

I texted Tristan, asking him to call me ASAP.

I sorrowfully imagined him on the witness stand, cleaning his oversized horn-rim glasses, a delaying tactic he often used to prepare his reply and avoid a stuttering answer. His childhood syndrome more or less conquered, he now spoke slowly and carefully, often beginning his sentences with an "Eh" pause—a whiz in the lab, but a reluctant witness in court.

My phone, still in hand, pinged with a message from my boss.

'*UR late. I have another meeting. I dropped a new CC file on yr desk.*'

I suspected that Jean was planning to bury me with cold case files so that I wouldn't have time to poke my nose into the Aldo murder.

* * *

I was stuck on a congested side street, biding my time, and enjoying a John Scofield CD. In an attempt to go around a flooded underpass, I, and a bevy of late-getting-to-work drivers, had all opted for this shortcut. It had now turned into a parking lot. The Jeep's hands-free system suddenly muted my jazz and showed a call from an unknown number.

Thinking it may be a contact with more information on Aldo's murder. I touched the answer symbol.

"Lieutenant Beaudry. Talk to me."

"Beaudry, this is Inspector Derek Henschel, CISC. We met on a case involving terrorists."

"Derek, the RCMP guy? You had me in handcuffs. What am I accused of now?"

"Forget that little incident. I'm with Criminal Intelligence Service now. We're sending this information through normal channels, but I figured I owed you one."

"No. I think we ended up in a tie game, but I always appreciate information. What is this about?"

"Last Thursday evening, there was a storm in Paris."

"Yeah, it's pouring in Montreal today. They must have sent it here."

"*As I was saying*, a flash flood unearthed the body of a local notary. He had been hastily planted in his own flower bed. A mister Laveredeere."

"Laverdière," I corrected. "You want me to go to Paris to solve a murder case?"

"Don't flatter yourself, Beaudry. We know who the murderer is."

"I don't understand. What has this to do with me?"

"I see you haven't changed. Your mouth is as fast as your gun. Never mind correcting my pronunciation. Shut up and listen."

"I'm all ears."

"The French police estimate that the notary was strangled Wednesday, late afternoon or early evening.

Surprisingly, Laverdeer left Paris *this Friday*, on Air France flight three-forty-four headed to Montreal."

"Somebody is using his passport," I said. "I still don't get what I can do about it."

"We think that the Mascara Man snuffed the notary, disguised himself as Laverdeer, and is in Montreal on a mission."

"Whoa horsey, back up a step. *Mascara man*?"

"An international hit-man, with at least eight known victims. Very slippery. The only intel we have on him is that he's Algerian, from the city of Mascara."

"I have a recent murder. The vic was shot with a twenty-two magnum. I found that unusual. Is that part of his M.O.?"

"Absolutely not him. His moniker is not only his place of birth, but also his modus operandi. He's a master of make-up and disguise. Moreover, his hits are camouflaged as accidental deaths. He may assassinate someone in your city and you will never know it."

"Ah, rats. I'm faced with an invisible man killing undetectably. Thanks for the heads-up. You really brightened up this rainy day."

"Anything for a fellow officer. I'll text you a picture of Laverdeer."

When again I corrected his pronunciation, he hung up.

* * *

An hour of splashing traffic and construction detours later, I stepped into my office to find a fluorescent pink message sticker, ticked off as urgent, plastered onto my monitor screen. The number belonged to Dobson's cell.

- 5 -

I slid to the side the fat file that my boss had so generously plopped on my desk, and returned Dobson's call.

"I know you're busy in court. Thanks for calling me back promptly,"

"Eh, what? I called you. All hell has, eh, broken loose here in the courthouse."

"I haven't heard anything about the courthouse. Has there been an escape? I just wanted to talk to you about the Aldo case."

"I, I think, Judge Collier, was assassinated in his chambers. I was attending him when he died."

"You think? What do you mean, you think?"

"Eh, we were waiting for the session to open when a clerk rushed in asking if there was a doctor in the courtroom."

"I presume you volunteered."

"The judge was slumped on a sofa, holding his chest. He mumbled, 'stabbed, stabbed,' before he passed out. There were no wounds or blood. Eh, it looked like an infarct. I tried everything I could, but to no avail. Same with the ambulance team. They couldn't bring him back. His clerk said the judge had a history of heart problems."

"Where does 'assassinated' come in?" I asked.

"I finally found a trace of blood above his left knee. My, eh… my thought, would be a needle puncture. I think someone gave him an overdose of adrenaline. The autopsy will tell me more."

"Hang on for a second. I've got a call from the boss on the other line."

The Captain's voice was apoplectic. He wanted me in his office now.

I thumbed back to Dobson. "If you hadn't been in court today, it would have passed as an unfortunate heart attack. I have to hang up. The boss is having a fit. I best see what he wants. Text me when you get back to the lab."

* * *

As requested, I trotted to the Captain's office. My foot was barely over the threshold when he stung me with another of his mock French swearwords.

"*Sacramentos*, you've contaminated Dobson. He's as hot-headed as you are. It appears I've let you work with him too often."

"Good morning, Jean. I was going to ask how you are, but your red face says it all."

"*Calvase*, I don't need your sarcasm. Poor Dobson may be facing charges."

"For trying to save the Judge?"

"No. For manhandling a secretary, and punching out a court clerk who tried to stop him from disrobing the stricken judge. How do you know about this already?"

"It's my job, remember? If there's a murder in this city, I know about it."

"Murder? What murder? The bailiff told me that the judge had a heart attack." The left side of Jean's mustache started to twitch. It looked like his fuzzy caterpillar was preparing to escape from under his nose.

Without asking permission, I moved one of his uncomfortable plastic visitor chairs closer to his desk, and sat down. By the time I finished my story of the RCMP phone call and of my conversation with Dobson, I had a smile on my face, and Jean's cheeks had toned down to a rosy pink. I walked out of the Captain's office with the mandate to follow up on Dobson's suspicions of foul play in the death of Judge Collier.

Jean had also kindly jogged my memory about the cold case that I was working on before my week's vacation.

"Before your enthusiasm for a new chase takes over. I'd like to remind you that I haven't seen a progress report on the burnt girl file. Did that stay on vacation, or did it come back to work with you?"

* * *

Back at my cubicle, I used Dobson's rendering to search for a comparative picture in our online missing persons' database. An hour-plus later, I had three potentials for the burnt girl. Pat, with her hacker skills, would have taken a mere five minutes to do the job. Thoughts of her kept creeping into my consciousness. There was an undeniable seed of worry about Pat germinating in the back of my brain. I couldn't put a name or a reason to it, but it was there. Bear, her pet nickname for me, reminded me of one of Winnie the Pooh's, sayings. 'Sometimes the smallest things take up the most room in your heart.'

My phone did its little chime sound, advising that I had a new text message. Dobson wrote that he was heading for his lab; they had released him from the courthouse. I pressed the call symbol, and left a voicemail asking him to meet me at *Bon Blé,* a Chinese restaurant a block away from headquarters. I added that this was important, and that, 'I don't have time for lunch,' his usual answer, was unacceptable.

Michael Kent

- 6 -

The trip from my East-end Major Crimes office to headquarters downtown took twenty minutes longer than I anticipated. The A720 expressway was down to one lane. The construction cones were on the job, but due to the rain, the construction workers were not.

I parked in the headquarters' lot, and umbrella in hand, hoofed it to the restaurant.

Dobson sat at a table close to the kitchen.

With his foot, he pushed the chair across from him out for me. "Thank you," he said.

"You're more than welcome. What did I do?"

"You spoke to the Captain. He called courthouse security and the clerk dropped the charges. They finally understood that evidence was fading with every lost minute. Eh, I had to examine the judge's body rapidly. It got his secretary upset."

"I understood from the Chief that you ripped off his clothes."

Like a scolded puppy, Tristan lowered his head and looked to one side.

The owner's wife came to present the menu. We ordered the special of the day, crispy beef with ginger and maple syrup on a bed of home-made noodles. A little of Quebec's maple industry had snuck into the Shanghai menu.

Dobson pushed his fork aside and bravely unwrapped and separated the chopsticks.

"Why did you want to meet?"

"I had an interesting call from an RCMP contact working in the Criminal Intelligence Service," I said. "He informed me that a hired assassin who makes his kills look like accidents is in town."

"Eh, you mean that the murder of the judge fits his M.O?"

"I respectfully suggest that you look into what cases Judge Collier was hearing. We may find a motive."

The little mound of noodles drooped off his chopsticks as Dobson nodded. "I'll text you and the Captain the list of his eh, cases. I'll also instruct my lab people to be on the lookout for any, any unusual detail on *all* autopsies while your assassin is about."

"There are international warrants out for the hit-man," I said. "They call him the Mascara Man, because he comes from an Algerian town of the same name, and also, because he uses make-up. He's a master of disguise."

"Eh, uses disguises, interesting detail. My team ran a scan of the court cameras for everyone entering the judge's chambers. There's a maintenance worker that nobody recognizes."

"Speaking of details, I'd appreciate anything you can give me on the Aldo case," I said. "Unofficially. When you have something. *If* you have something."

"You don't have to ask, Robert. I'll leave messages on your home phone."

I moved both bills to my side of the table.

Dobson mumbled, "Thank you."

I reached into my breast pocket, "No, I should be thanking you. Have a look at this."

I handed him the pictures of the three girls who most resembled his computer mock-up. He unfolded them and selected the last one.

"Place your thumb to hide the different hairdo," he said. "Same eye distance, same shape nose and cheek bone structure. Chances are this is her. Helen Fortier."

"I'll pick up a copy of the case file from Farrow at missing persons," I said.

Dobson put a twenty on the table. "I'll wager it's her."

I hoped he was right, but I put my twenty over his and told him to hold the bet. It would be a small price to pay for solving a year-old crime and, more importantly, get the boss off my back to get some free time to help my friend Nico.

* * *

Sergeant James Farrow could easily portray a WWII British officer in a play or motion picture. With his proper London accent, he'd jump grades and be cast as a major or a colonel. Slim and ramrod straight described him well. Salt and pepper hair and a well-groomed handlebar mustache completed the picture.

His rolled-up sleeves and a perilously high stack of files on his desk hinted at a busy day. He wasn't happy to see me.

"You'll pardon if I don't stand and salute, I'm a tad busy right now."

I pointed to the pile. "I'm a detective. I can deduce that from the clues."

"Inasmuch as you have neglected to make an appointment, I would venture to say that you are here to steal another file from us. Then bask in the limelight for solving another disappearance."

"To quote Vin Diesel, 'We all deal with being unfairly judged,'" I said. "If you can spare some time maybe we can team up on this one."

I handed him the composite and the picture of Helen Fortier from the missing person posting.

"Doctor Dobson from CSI bet me a twenty that this is the girl found last year in a shallow grave by the railroad tracks."

"Well, I'd not wager against him. Rumor has it that when he's finished presenting his evidence, defence attorneys leave the courtroom in tears."

I borrowed a chair from the empty desk across from his, and sat down. "More fact than rumor," I said.

He studied the missing girl photo while absentmindedly finger-combing the left side of his elegant mustache.

"We found the body early last September, but your bulletin had her missing for some seven months before that."

As if he suddenly remembered something, he stood from his chair, and headed for a bank of filing cabinets. Over his shoulder he told me to wait.

I permitted myself a trip to the department's coffee machine. I dropped a loonie into the slot, punched in black-strong, and said a silent prayer. The first sip told me the brew wasn't half bad.

When I got back to Farrow's desk he was leafing through a skinny file folder.

"Not much of a file," I said, lifting my cup. "You want one?"

"Can't stand the stuff."

"It's better than the dishwater from the steampunk contraption in our office," I said.

He pulled out a yellow sheet from the folder. "This one rang a bell. A girl from a middle-class family, still living at home, a good student, never a problem child. She goes out clubbing with a dozen of her first-year university classmates. Somewhere in the hop from one downtown club to another, she disappears. It's only next morning when the parents start calling them that the friends realize she's gone."

"What rang the bell for you?"

"A couple of weeks later, one of her classmates reported that he saw her leaving a mid-town duplex and get into a white van. By the time he U-turned, the van was long gone. He took down the address."

"Who followed up?"

"The classmate was ambiguous, said it *looked* like her. We sent one of our new recruits. He interviewed Linda Weeks, a young woman at the given location. Presented with the photo of Fortier, she said her roommate had moved out and didn't leave a forwarding address."

"Roommate? You said Fortier was living with her parents."

"Ding-dong. You rang the bell."

"Another follow-up?" I asked.

"I knocked on the door, maybe a week later." James said. "No Linda Weeks, the home owner a refugee from Nigeria, a Mister Duff, was running a small delivery company from that location. He knew nothing about nothing. I called the young man that thought he saw her. He was now less than sure. End of follow-up."

James handed me the yellow paper. A note had been appended to the file by an observant beat cop. Over the last two years, nine parking violations were issued for a 1969 yellow and black side-striped Chevy Camaro. The owner, Bosede Duff, listed his residence at the address visited by Farrow.

"I think I hear the chime of another bell," I said.

"Loud and clear my friend. It would appear that the conveniently forgetful Mister Duff was living there when the young woman was questioned. I'd say we are due for another visit."

* * *

Forty-five minutes later, James was driving us to the Bosede Duff address. The original file showed her roommate, Linda Weeks, had been questioned—, but unexplainably, there was no mention of Mister Duff.

The neighbourhood comprised rows of copy-paste semi-detached, ugly pinkish-red brick duplexes, with on-street parking allowed on each side on alternating days. The Camaro was parked one house down from our target address.

"Our man is home," I said.

James nodded. "A classic muscle car. Bloody shame about the rusted bonnet and dented side panel."

I pointed to a fire hydrant space. "Park here." James politely refused. The rain had stopped. "Fine day," he remarked, as we strolled the two blocks from where he had finally backed in our unmarked car.

Out of habit, I touched the hood and grill of the Camaro as we passed it.

"Cooled off I'm sure," James said.

I nodded. "Warmed by the sun, not motor heat."

"Been here for a while," he said. "It's leaking green radiator coolant. Shameful maintenance."

"You okay to take point?" I asked. "I've been told that I'm as wide as I am tall. It seems to put people on edge when I fill up the doorway."

"My pleasure. I take it this is a courtesy visit."

"Let's… play it by ear."

"From your tone, perhaps we should call for support," James said.

I flipped open my raincoat, flashing the CZ85 Combat in my shoulder rig.

"This is all the back-up we need."

"Not a regulation firearm, I see. That's worrisome. I'm rethinking our partnership," James said as we mounted the steps.

"I like what your Winston Churchill wrote. 'When I look back on all these worries, I remember the story of the old man who said on his deathbed that he had had a lot of trouble in his life, most of which had never happened.'"

"I wouldn't have thought of you as a reader of Winston's writing."

"I don't read books. I devour them."

James rang the bell twice in a series of three dashes. I stood behind and slightly to his right by the hinge side of the door.

A minute later, a purple-haired girl with a thirteen-year-old face and a twenty-year-old body cracked open the door. Barefoot, she wore a tight blouse and a shorter-than-short skirt. Or maybe it was just a wide belt. Her lips were puffy and day-glow pink, her false eyelashes a little askew. She also sported a painful looking purple bruise under her left eye, and red choke marks on both sides of her neck. Her appearance announced abuse.

When James showed her his badge, her face drained to a light shade of scared, and silent tears flowed down her cheeks.

My situational awareness clicked into danger mode. Hidden behind James, I unholstered my weapon, and held it down along my leg.

"May we come in, dear?" James asked as he slid his hand towards his belt and holster.

Her eyes flicked left to something hidden behind the door. Lips trembling, she shook her head slowly.

James repositioned himself farther to the left.

"We just need a moment of your time. We would like to talk to you about Miss Linda Weeks. She used to live at this address."

From my side and position, I saw above the young girl. A framed wall mirror to her right reflected the image behind the door. A wiry spiked-haired black man held a shotgun in the crook of his arm.

I yelled, "Gun!" slamming my shoulder into the door and stiff-arming Purple-hair. She landed on her butt in the hallway, next to the shotgun dude that had been thrown backwards by the swing of the door.

He pulled the trigger without aiming. The birdshot took a half-moon chunk out of the doorframe, inches above James's head. When the guy racked the shotgun for a second try, I didn't say 'police, put up your hands,' nor 'drop it.' I pumped two fast rounds towards him. One went through his right biceps and the other channelled into the gunstock.

James put a hole somewhere close to Mister Shotgun's appendix. The man yapped a good imitation of someone stepping on a Pomeranian's paw. He fell heavily to the floor, still making wounded dog sounds. The twelve-gauge skittered to my feet on the hardwood.

I picked it up and turned to James. "Never a dull moment, partner."

James had a grin on his kisser that put the Cheshire Cat to shame. The ends of his handlebar mustache curled out; it looked like a double fuzzy hard-on.

Michael Kent

- 7 -

James's bullet had punched in and out of Mister Shotgun's right side love handle with little damage. A dishtowel tied around his biceps took care of the dripping blood from that more open wound. We used Duff's belt and James's cuffs to hog-tie him and lock him to an old-fashioned cast iron radiator.

I advised blubbering Purple-hair that she was not under arrest, but that she was being detained. I moved her to the kitchen and handcuffed her to another radiator.

Before we cleared the house, we called the precinct, requested back-up, and an *Urgences-Santé* ambulance.

The basement had been sectioned into four cells, a TV room, and a laundry area. All the windows were boarded and barred. In one of the locked bedrooms, we found Maria Sanchez, a voluptuous illegal alien from Argentina. She had raven black hair down to her mid-back and wore a tattered old-fashioned flowery house-coat that still managed to reveal that she had curves in all the right places. She also had similar red choke marks around her neck and a puffed-up bottom lip that didn't prevent her from talking a mile a minute, berating us for not having found and freed her weeks ago.

Back in the kitchen she continued her harangue for our slow police work, and for only wounding and not killing her pig of a captor outright.

She calmed down when I cuffed her to the drippy-eyed purple-haired girl.

Within a few minutes, two colourful patrol teams arrived. The officers wore camouflage pants in mottled gray, pink or loden green instead of their uniform trousers. The rank and file were using this dress-down ploy to protest stalled negotiations with the city, over wages and proposed cuts to their pension plan.

They rechecked every nook and cranny of the house while we questioned the women. The purple-haired, tearful Laurie, and Maria Sanchez, both gave us the same story.

Over the last twenty-four months, with the help of Rohypnol, street named Mexican Valium, or rope, the date rape drug, half a dozen girls had been kidnapped from various downtown clubs or open parties and forced into prostitution. This house was one of three they knew of. Shotgun man, Bosede Duff, had two partners who took shifts to keep the girls obedient and move them between 'dates', or to other houses or apartments used as brothels.

Laurie had been captive for over a year and recognized the picture of our missing girl, Helen Fortier.

"I remember her from one of the other houses. She was very kind to me and she seemed to take care of the other girls."

Between crying jags, Laurie told us that the 'boss' of the other house was a sadist who kept everyone in line, with a bit of torture and regular beatings.

The paramedics had temporarily patched up Duff. He lay on a stretcher in the hallway. I moved closer and—accidently—leaned on his punctured arm while asking if he had killed Helen Fortier. In a pause between his swearing and moaning, he gave up one of his partners.

"I never touched her. She was in Gerry's stable. Ask *him* how he dumped the crazy bitch."

I pressed video record on my phone, aimed it at Duff then panned to Laurie and Maria, asking them what they knew of the murder of Helen.

In the background Duff was threatening death to both of them. Maria spat in his direction, and confirmed that Duff had implicated one of his partners Gerry Nichols, nicknamed 'Pickles', in the death of Helen Fortier. She also said that Duff had helped bury the body, and threatened that the same fate would befall them if they tried to escape. Then she gave us the addresses of the two other houses that she had been driven to.

"For your sake, Bosede, I hope the court doesn't grant you bail," I said, "If they do, I might just give your picture and coordinates to the families of missing girls. Just saying."

Past due to report in, I called my boss.

"Just to let you know, I've assisted Sergeant James Farrow on a missing person's case that's tied in with the murder of Helen Fortier—the burnt body found last year next to the railroad tracks."

"If you called to tell me that you're helping another department, you can submit your expense account to them, not to me."

"Ah...not exactly the reason I phoned. There were shots fired. I wanted to advise you before Internal Affairs rattles your cage."

I learned another three French swear words from my boss. But, in an unusual fit of protective behaviour, Jean said he would send a police union rep to the scene.

* * *

When the Infernal Affairs team of Lorne Trehearne and his rotund partner Simon arrived, the apartment looked like an out-of-control party. Two patrolmen and a Mutt and Jeff ambulance tech team were jostling a wheeled gurney down the stairs. Duff, handcuffed to the metal sides, still swearing and complaining, was headed to the hospital.

The police union representative hovered close to me. He nibbled on a doughnut and sipped a coffee from the stack of goodies that he had thoughtfully brought from the local fast food emporium. In the kitchen, two social workers and a female officer were talking to Laurie and Maria. Kevin Connor from Dobson's Forensic Identification unit was busy taking evidence pictures and flirting with a female patrol officer. A SWAT coordinator, speaking on a two-way radio, relayed the building layouts, which both girls had given him, to his commander, who had his team ready to pounce on the other brothels. James was on the phone bragging to one of his partner detectives from Missing Persons about how in one raid he would close many of their open files.

I pointed the Infernal team to the living room and sat in the wing chair, leaving them the stained sofa. The union rep stood leaning against the back of my chair, sipping his second coffee.

As usual, Trehearne had his trusty aluminum clipboard and pen at the ready to record any procedural peccadillo he could nail me with. I gave them my story, told them that Detective James Farrow was in charge of the case, and, notwithstanding vociferous objections from the ferret-faced Trehearne, I left the party.

- 8 -

It was a quarter to suppertime when I left the scene—too late to go back to the office. Anxious to head home, I aimed my Jeep toward my downtown condo. My timing was bad. At this time of day, I was in *rush*-hour traffic, an obvious misnomer. At the speed we were now motoring, a nonchalant escargot would have zipped by me. Fifty cars ahead, large flashing lights in the shape of an arrow pointed left, enforced and supported by a legion of orange construction cones which herded three lanes of traffic into a bottleneck. Why the city had decided to repair *all* its infrastructures in the same year was beyond me.

I checked my missed calls and messages on the car's screen. When I'm on the job, my phone is off or on mute. Years ago, I heard the story of a detective whose phone rang while he was searching a house. An escaped felon hiding in the next room put four .357 slugs through the plasterboard wall where the sound came from. The detective survived, but he still walks with a slight limp. Lesson learned.

I took the message from Pat first. The system's synthetic female voice read the text. "I'm busy until late tonight. If I can, I'll try and call you." I was missing Pat, and itching to ask what was bothering her. The dull electronic voice didn't help the tone of the curt message. The worry seed in the back of my brain was now budding tiny leaves. The second message was from Dobson stating that he would call me later.

*　*　*

The lengthy traffic crawl, plus the terse message from Pat had upset me. Back at my apartment, my mood dropped another notch to sombre. Home from a week's vacation, I hadn't yet refilled my larder. The fridge was empty. My hungry stomach would have to wait its turn while I dealt with a cat-mischief clean-up. This morning, I'd left in a rush, and had forgotten to remove the toilet paper roll or put the cat out. Like a Halloween prank, the hall and bathroom were decorated in shreds of double–ply, kitteny-soft tissue. Crackers, his front paws curled under him, lay on the kitchen table, staring at me in faked innocence as I squatted to pick up his handiwork.

When I asked, "Why do you do this?" he ran off to hide in the bedroom.

I had cleaned up the first mess and had just discovered the mangled toothpaste tube and paw prints in the bathroom sink, when my home phone rang. I rushed to the kitchen hoping it was Pat. But an unknown number showed on the little screen.

"Beaudry here. Talk to me."

"D-Dobson here. I left a message."

"I was expecting your call. Do you have anything on Aldo's murder?"

"Eh, from the powder residue on his neck we figure the assailant rested the rifle barrel on the edge of the window and fired three rapid shots all in the same spot."

"Rifle?"

"Yes, firing twenty-two magnum forty grain soft points. The expanding bullets made a mess of the spinal cord between C2 and C3. Oh, we also found bike tire tracks in the grass along the driver's side."

"The murderer used a bicycle as his escape vehicle?"

"Eh…my team said it looks like an off-road motorcycle."

"This is getting stranger by the minute. Anything else?"

"Yes, yes, very…"

"Very? More strange stuff on Aldo?"

"Eh, no, Judge Collier was murdered. The tox report indicates he received ten to eleven times the recommended dosage for Epinephrine."

"No surprise."

"The surprise is, eh, I went through Collier's files and found that Sydney Scheiner, was one of the defence attorneys on an ongoing case before the judge."

"What's that got to do with anything?"

"Eh, Scheiner died of a presumed heart attack on Sunday morning."

"What was the case about?"

"A biker gang accused of extortion and drug trafficking. Eh, the case wasn't going well for them."

"You could be right," I said. "Unhappy with the potential results, the gang may have decided to fire their lawyer permanently, and change the judge."

"And, and, remove unfavorable testimony. Eh, late last night, one of the four witnesses against them was victim of a hit and run."

"Dobson, once is fate, twice is a pattern, and three times is a conspiracy. You've just confirmed that the Mascara Man is doing business in town. Can you get an autopsy done on Scheiner? We've got to get our invisible hit-man off the streets."

"No, religious beliefs dictate that the body should be intact for the burial, and no embalming. I did get permission for a blood sample. The report will probably be available late tomorrow."

Dobson said the biker gang was part of the Rock Machine. I thanked him and promised to keep him in the loop on my search for the Mascara Man.

By the time, I finished the cat clean up I was way past due for supper, and beginning to eye Cracker's filled bowl with envy. I opted for my closest local French bistro.

I needed to know if the word was on the street about another gunsel in town. I called Antonio, a retired hit-man. Years ago, I had 'gone off the reservation,' and gone after a group of international terrorists. I fast wound up outgunned and he had offered to help me pull my chestnuts out of the fire. "I'm retired, not dead," was his comment.

He answered on the second ring.
"I'm surprised you picked up. I was expecting to leave a message."
"Saw your number. What do you want?"
"I'm headed to Luc's bistro. You want to join me?"
"You're paying?"
"Sure."

"Ah, are we discussing something interesting?"

"Usual bullshit and some business."

"You need business advice?"

"Always appreciated."

"Do I need to take notes?"

"No."

Antonio said, "Thirty minutes," and hung up.

He had taught me his unique coded language. The bullshit and business meant smelly business, murder and mayhem. Advice meant that he would be involved, and the reference to notes meant bringing something with him—weapons or more muscle.

* * *

Antonio sat across from me, facing as always, the front of the restaurant. Satiated, he passed on the dessert, opting for a snifter of Rainwater Madeira.

I succumbed to one of Luc's sweet pastries.

I tilted my head toward a young couple, the only other patrons left in the restaurant at this late hour.

"I think he's working up his courage to ask her to marry him," I said.

Antonio flicked his dark eyes to the right.

"He doesn't have to worry about the answer. She's looking at him like you're looking at your fluffy *profiterole*."

During the meal, I told him about the Mascara Man and Dobson's suspicions that he had already eliminated three people for a local biker gang, and that the invisible killer may have three more witnesses in his sights.

Antonio was miffed that some outsider had taken contracts in Montreal and he didn't know about it. For Antonio, *officially* retired didn't mean that he was out of the loop, nor that he wished to be.

"My boss gave me the okay to look into this, but I'd prefer the unofficial route. I don't have a formal plan as yet, but I know I'm going to need some invisible help to find my invisible man. It's going to be difficult, if not impossible, to link him with the local crimes. And, based on the record of our lenient judges, I'd prefer to turn him over to the RCMP and Interpol. They don't care if he's breathing or not."

"I like a plan with some flexibility," Antonio said.

When I paid the bill, I had a dangerous partner on board.

Michael Kent

- 9 -

I rose, devitalized from a toss-and-turn night, but with the framework of a plan taking shape in my mind. I ambled to my mini-gym in the spare bedroom and did some stretches and my tai-chi routine. During *Parting Wild Horse's Mane*, something thudded to the floor in the living room. It didn't have the tinkle of breaking glass or pottery, so I ignored it. I was more worried about Pat not calling me last night than I was about my crazy cat's antics.

When I stepped out of the shower, I found a perforated and twisted tube of toothpaste on the floor and Crackers stretched over the vessel sink, licking the mint taste off my toothbrush.

It appeared that his mood today was what Pat called his mix of hooliganism, shenanigans, and mischievousness.

"What are you doing, you monster?" My loud question got him on the run with my toothbrush in his maw. I hoped my morning cat problems were not foreshadowing the rest of my day.

I texted Pat. I wrote that I was worried about her, and asked if she was okay. I ended with a series of heart emoticons and X's. She'd probably wonder if it was really me or if someone had hacked my phone. During my sappy texting, Crackers traded my mangled toothbrush for a half strip of bacon.

I then texted my RCMP contact, Derek, and brought him up to speed on our trail of the Mascara Man and his probable recent kills. As I ended my message, the phone showed a new and unwanted note. An invitation from Sergeant Trehearne of Internal Affairs for a sit-down tomorrow afternoon.

At my last sip of coffee, my phone played the drum roll announcing my boss. The disappointment of it not being Pat reflected in my tone of voice.

"Yeah."

"You sound in a lousy mood. This should cheer you up. The Duff guy is practicing for the opera. The prosecutor is trading his expired Nigerian visa and an outstanding warrant from France for testimony against the rest of his gang. They're working out a plea bargain."

"So he gets to stay in a *nice* Canadian jail," I said. "What happened with the SWAT team raid?"

"They found six missing girls, one doped up and in pretty bad shape, and apparently all of the kidnap gang. Farrow is basking in his success, and you're getting the credit for solving the burnt body murder."

"Helen Fortier," I said.

"Who?"

"The burnt body wasn't just a body—she was a young woman. Her name was Helen Fortier. Did you send somebody to tell her parents?"

"CC and a social worker will take care of it this morning."

"I'm following a lead on the Mascara Man," I said. "I won't be in the office today."

"Good, I prefer you out of the office when you're bad tempered and testy. I put another cold file on your desk, and your paperwork is piling up. Please note that I'm not authorizing overtime for the rest of the month. Have a good day." The Captain hung up.

O'Neil, a stickler for protocol, always respects the rulebook. He's good with the paperwork, but poor with people skills. He has no sense of humor or any patience. I always get a fast comeback when I speak to him with attitude. He also has a few chauvinistic brain cells under his military-cut gray hair. He's all for women's equality, but always sends CC, Carol Curran, the only female in the homicide squad, to do the bad news house-calls.

I had her number on speed-dial. Before my tumble for Pat, Carol and I had an ongoing office flirtation.

When she answered, I said, "I heard the boss volunteered you again. I just wanted to give you some thoughts on Helen and wish you good courage. Better you than me. After seventeen years on the force, the bad news job still makes me shudder."

"Beaudry, you're ruining your tough guy reputation with me. I think your heart is wider than your shoulders."

"Don't spread any nasty rumors, or I'll tell everyone that I have a pair of your panties under my bed."

"You wish. Besides, it would get you in trouble with your tall redhead."

"She's not around these days. In Quebec again."

"Well if you get lonely, call me anytime. I may not even wear panties."

"Tempting, but that's not why I called. Helen was a fighter. She was killed because the criminals couldn't break her spirit. She kept trying to escape. She took care of the other girls when she could. She comforted and encouraged them not to give up hope.

A small consolation to her family, but if it wasn't for her death, we would not have saved eight young girls from the clutches of those pimps."

"You're waxing poetic, Beaudry. You had better stop before you bring a tear to my eye. You sure you're okay?"

"Not to worry, I'll make up for my tender moment later today. I'm about to unsheathe the sword of justice against an ill-reputed biker gang."

Carol said thanks for the info on Helen, and made the sound of make-believe kisses before hanging up.

Last night, on an entirely different and more serious vein, I had promised to call Antonio with a plan of action. He was always ready to jump in if there was a chance of gunplay involved.

I dialed his number. His answering service never used an outgoing message; it just beeped, and then you had a mere ten seconds to leave your number. He'd respond if and when it pleased him.

Forty minutes later when Antonio called, I was on the mission to re-stock my pantry, squeezing tomatoes in the produce aisle of my local food market.

"You at headquarters? Can you talk?"

"Grocery shopping. I'm avoiding a pile of dumb reports on my desk today. I'm all ears."

We set up an end-of-afternoon meeting in the back room of a downtown health club where he was part owner, and where I often worked out.

- 10 -

I had sweated through a fast fifty-minute weight session and was pounding the hell out of an Everlast 70 pound MMA bag when Antonio stepped up behind me.

"You working out some frustrations, Beaudry?"

"My girlfriend is out of town. This is better than a cold shower."

"She better come home soon, or I'll have to charge you for a replacement bag. Get cleaned up. I'll wait in the back office."

* * *

Antonio sat behind his battered gray metal desk. His normally close shaved head showed a bit of salt and pepper fuzz above his ears. I was about to comment on the need for a trim, but his mouth was a smile-less line and his black eyes cold and emotionless. His usual deadly look preempted my comment.

"Nobody in my circle of business knows about this rogue hit-man," he said. "He's stepping on the toes of some dangerous people. Operating in our town without permission is a major affront. You better have a good plan, or else I may just go after him myself."

I took another sip of the spiked coffee that he had poured.

"I always appreciate your help Antonio. We get along like old friends. Don't spoil it by coming out of retirement. Be patient, we may wind up facing the Mascara Man together. First, we have to find him."

"Apart from antagonizing me, what's your plan to find Mister invisible killer?"

"From the choice of victims, it looks like he's in the hire of a local chapter of the Rock Machine motorcycle gang."

"They're loose associates of the family I used to work for," Antonio said. "Strange they didn't go for local talent."

"I'd say they didn't want their involvement known. The deaths were supposed to look like accidents. It was their pure bad luck that a CSI cop was on the scene. We need to find out who gave out the contract and how he communicates with Mascara Man."

"Okay hot-shot, tell me how exactly you're going to get a gang of hardened bikers to roll over and give you that info?"

"We fight fire with fire. We get a rival gang to help us kidnap the Sergeant-at-Arms of the Rock Machine."

"Kidnap the head enforcer for the gang—that's whacko. Have you gone senile, Beaudry?"

"No, just desperate to get this schmuck off the streets. My unblemished reputation is at stake."

"Unblemished?"

"I always nail the criminal," I said. "The rule book comes in second."

"Yadda, yadda, yadda. I'm waiting for your sales pitch. You know that your rulebook states that any evidence you collect by illegal means is tainted and non-admissible in court."

I took another sip of my strengthened coffee.

"Yup, I know the fruit-of-the-poison-tree rule by heart. I'm not looking for an arrest. As I told you, I have an RCMP officer with a stack of international warrants in his back pocket. I just have to deliver a body. I get more brownie points if we deliver a vertical one, but that'll depend on Mascara's mood."

Antonio added another shot of cognac to the dregs of his coffee. "I'm still listening."

"On the premise that the enemy of my enemy is my friend, my plan is to get the Red Devils on my side to screw up the Rock Machine, who've had the big end of the stick for years."

"I agree that if—*if* the Rock Machine did hire Mascara, the head enforcer would surely know about it, and the Red Devils would be pleased to get away with some dirty deeds against their rivals while having a homicide detective in their debt."

"I wouldn't be in their debt. It's my way of apologizing. We'd be even-steven."

"Apologizing?"

"That's where you come in," I said. "I recently had a slight altercation with some gang hangers-on during an arrest. They may be gunning for me."

"Your slight altercation, I presume, is what I saw on the tube a few days ago. The newscaster said one of them will need substantial dental surgery."

"Well, he tried a karate kick to my balls. It got me a bit peeved. In a tit-for-tat, I fed him a pool ball. I heard rumors that his buddies are now gunning for me."

"Ah, the big guy needs protection. I always enjoy riding shotgun. The first shots are always in the direction of the driver."

From my jacket pocket, I laid out the rough sketch I made when I cased the pool hall/bar prior to my arrest of Albert Brody, and my run-in with the bikers.

"I figure we can come in by the loading dock." Before I could elaborate, Antonio snatched the plan to his side of the desk. "How many goons and guns will be in the place?"

"From my past surveillance, I'd say nine to twelve of both."

"No good. If we come in by the back, it'll look like a surprise attack. All hell will break loose. I can take out maybe six, so we need another player on our team."

"Hey, I can cover three or four, no problem."

"Not with an empty gun you can't."

"What?"

"You make a wide target, Beaudry. If you don't want to come out of this with holes in your hide, we do it my way."

Antonio broke down his plan for me. It was risky, but operationally sound. For me, gunplay was a last resort. For Antonio, it was a skill set.

He would need a day to recruit another shooter for our team. We agreed to hit the biker pool hall the next evening.

Michael Kent

- 11 -

I had worked up an appetite at the gym, and I headed homeward to whip up supper and feed my crazy cat. I didn't make it.

Halfway to my apartment, I hit a human wall of student protesters blocking the streets south of Saint Catherine. The cooking-pot-banging procession was corralled by riot-garbed, clown-trouser'ed patrol officers. Objection to the announced increase in university fees was the march of the day. Tomorrow would probably be the ecology minded and the First Nations opposition to a proposed western pipeline. It was the summer parades of discontent.

I also was displeased. The congestion meant I'd have to make a long detour, and my stomach was talking to me in ever-increasing growls. It claimed an immediate need of sustenance. I was close to the Eaton Center and their extensive food court. From the corner of my eye, I spotted a departing mini-van two cars from the street corner. I whipped around a hesitant taxi driver and slid into the space. My stock-car maneuver ended in perfect harmony with the angry beep of his horn.

The food court reflected cosmopolitan Montreal; it offered everything in eats, from specialty popcorn and pretzels, to Greek, Italian, Japanese, Chinese, Thai, Lebanese, and Vietnamese, in addition to the usual fast food chains.

Pat watched her diet, as well as policing mine. Today, I was taking a break. I chose a loaded double burger, cheesed and chipotle-sauced, and added a side of onion rings. To my credit, it was free-range beef sans steroids.

Blank-eyed teens thumbing their smart phones roamed the mall in packs. A waste of their summer in this air-conditioned, artificial environment.

I'd been raised on a farm by my father and his brother, so my formative years were the antithesis of this stale urban scene. The beef guarantee logo on my food wrapper brought back memories of our milk cattle herd, open fields, and the intoxicating smell of fresh cut hay.

I'd lost my mother the week before my eighth birthday. She was a collateral victim in a botched bank robbery. My immature mind couldn't accept her disappearance, and I acted out in frustration and grief. My dad, busy with the farm, the housework, and suffering his own angst, could no longer handle my attitude, and my danger-prone actions.

The week after I crashed the tractor and fractured my wrist, my uncle came to live with us. Ostensibly, to control me. He did much more.

Uncle Bruno was a living example of a man's man. His strong will and energy permitted no defeat. Disasters turned into new opportunities; nothing seemed to stop him. In the Vietnam War, he'd lost a foot to a land mine and a pretty wife to the handsome son of the local farm equipment dealer. As he must have done for himself, he turned my anger into a passion for hands-on work. A mechanic by trade, he shared his skills with me. We stripped the damaged tractor to the frame and rebuilt it. I started the project with complaints of bruised fingers and oil stained hands. By September, I was proud of the grime under my fingernails and of the John Deere 1530 that sparkled and purred like a showroom model.

By the end of my teenage years, I excelled in hand-to-hand combat, and had acquired expert-level mechanic, carpentry, and hunting skills.

My reminiscing bubble popped when my phone played its tune.

Dobson's number flashed on the screen.

"Is this bad news?"

"No, eh, lawyer Scheiner had the same overdose as the judge. We're labeling it a suspicious death for now. Eh, someone in the RCMP put pressure on the lab to, eh, expedite the tests. Would you know anything about that?"

"Absotively not, and even if I did, I couldn't tell you."

"Absotively?"

"Absolutely added to a positively," I said.

"The Captain said you're following a lead on the Mascara Man."

"Tomorrow will be a busy day. I'm attending the funeral for Nico's cousin in the morning, then I have to suffer an Internal Affairs meeting with Lorn, and then I have a conclave with the Red Devils bikers, and that can go two ways. They may shoot me or help me with information on Mascara."

"Robert Beaudry, you better be careful. I'm scared that one day you'll wind up on my autopsy table. I don't think I could take that."

"Aww, I didn't know you cared, Tristan."

"I'm serious. You're one of the only detectives that keeps me informed on his cases. For the others, I'm still just a lab rat. I give them evidence and I never hear anything until I see a capture on the news."

"*If* you see a capture. We don't solve everything."

"*You* do."

"Just doing my job. I graduated the academy with the intention of putting *all* the bad guys behind bars, or in the ground."

"A bad cliché," Dobson said. "You sound like a cartoon character sometimes."

"You once told me about the difficult times you had in your youth because of your sexual orientation. I guess I still have demons from my youth. Let's leave it at that."

Before he hung up, Dobson mentioned that he'd attend the funeral tomorrow. Nico also appreciated Dobson and his CSI team.

By the time I got my back to my 4x4 the streets had cleared. My phone rang before I drove out. It was Pat's number. I killed the ignition with one hand as I swiped the green answer icon with the other.

"Hi."

"I'm disturbing you, am I? I hear a lot of background noises."

"I'm in the car, and I'm only disturbed by the lack of your presence."

"I gleaned that from your text this morning. Have ya gone soft?"

"Not sure if you're referring to my head or something else. I do plead guilty to an attack of missing you."

"That's good to hear, but you'd best toughen up, bucko. I need a strong shoulder to lean on. This job's turned into a holy show."

"Oh. I thought you were having misgivings about our relationship."

"Not at all, at all, ye bleeding doope ya."

"Do you want to talk about it?" I said. "I'd drive up to see you, but that'd be a six hour stint because I have the funeral early tomorrow morning."

"I'm scarlet for not being there. Give my regrets and condolences to Nico. I've a breakfast meet with my boss. I can't put this off any longer. It's been eating away at me for weeks now. I'm going to tell him this job is banjaxed. I'm not a real cop anymore. I work my arse off to discover evidence, but it doesn't mean a thing because we never actually prosecute the tossers. I'm just a spoke turning with the wheel. It's all just a big political show."

Pat spent the next seventeen minutes venting her frustrations. It was a sure sign she was very upset or mad when she fell back into Dublin expressions. I was glad just to hear her voice and flattered that she wanted my opinion on her life choices. The bottom line was that she felt as if she now worked for a collection agency, and no longer an arm of the law.

"When Commissioner Martin recruited me, he said the Anti-Corruption Squad would make sweeping changes," Pat said. "The only sweeping we've done is brush back stolen money into the Provincial coffers."

"I've heard something like three hundred million," I said. "That's more than a dustpan full."

"That's only a small part of what was stolen over the years, and the crooked politicians and money grubbing contractors get off with a slap on the wrist when they return part of their ill-gotten gains. The average jail sentence in the rare instance where we do prosecute is under eighteen months."

"I think the public is behind you on that. The expression *crime doesn't pay* should be changed to violent crime doesn't pay, but white collar crime pays handsomely."

Pat sighed in frustration. "I spent three months digging evidence on a city engineer who was taking bribes to swing road contracts toward a group of colluding contractors. From my estimates, I figured to the tune of over four million dollars. In the end, he gave back two and a half million, pleaded no contest and had his license suspended for five months. I'm after telling you, it's all a bad joke."

"I'll back you up on anything you decide, Pat. You know that."

"I'm planning to call my old boss at the Fraud Squad to see if he wants me back."

"I'm sure your old team would love to have you and your hacking skills. What does your gut tell you?"

"My gut doesn't tell me anything, but my heart says two weeks' vacation and then the Fraud Squad."

"Sounds like a plan. Winona, one of your favorite actresses said, 'It's all about knowing when to listen to that internal conversation and—without sounding really hokey—when to tune it out and follow your heart.'"

I suggested a few weekend plans and we hung up without me telling her about my convocation to the IA office, nor my meeting tomorrow with the bikers.

Knowing that back home I'd face a hostile and hungry twenty-pound Maine Coon, I stopped at a *dépanneur* for some fresh milk, and a couple cans of his favorite fishy-food treat.

- 12 -

It was readily apparent that Nico's cousin was a well-known chef, a sociable restaurant owner, and a respected businessman in the Italian community. The church was packed. Although I got there early, I wound up in the fourth row from the rear in an aisle side bench.

A Mediterranean funeral is often replete with flowers. For today's ceremony, it seemed as if the mourners had raided Montreal's renowned botanical garden. The air reeked of sweet perfume. The respectful bouquet I had sent yesterday was lost in a tropical jungle.

More and more people packed in behind the pews and overflowed to the church entrance.

Some ten minutes later, the standing crowd parted for the cross-bearing altar boy that led the procession of priest, more altar boys, pallbearers pushing the coffin on a gilded and flowered trolley, and family.

The widow wore the traditional all-black, ankle-length dress plus a veil. Adrianna, the rebellious daughter, wore a simple grey jumper and white blouse, both colors in stark contrast to her red eyes and nose. Aldo's sister Annick and her consort followed.

The handsome gene in Nico's bloodline was strong. Annick's new pixie haircut nicely framed her already spectacular features. She walked with a hip swishing flow that reminded me of a Shakira dance move. The man whose arm she clung to was another stark contrast; Swarthy and mean-eyed well defined his appearance. He had a permanent 'you looking at me' scowl on his kisser. He was one of Nico's relatives rumored to work on the other side of the badge.

I didn't recognize anyone else in the DiLalla clan. Both Nico and Carmen nodded hello to me as they passed. His daughters floated down the aisle, empty looks on their faces, as if they were in a trance. As soon as the coffin stopped at the front of the church, the wailing commenced.

I wondered if the family had rented professional mourners or his daughter Adrianna, had tuned the tap to "on" again.

Two-and-a-quarter hours later, the priest blessed the attendance, and people followed the coffin out to the rear of the church, all in sequence, starting from the first rows. On the premise that Aldo's murder was of a personal nature, I held my phone to my chest and discreetly filmed everyone as they walked up the aisle in my direction. One never knows.

As I turned to leave, I saw Sergeant Lamont, Nico's partner, standing behind the last row of pews, a carry-on suitcase at his feet.

He joined me as I walked out.

Roger glanced at the phone in my hand, "Please send me a copy of that."

"You don't miss much," I said. "You just got back?"

"Two hours ago. I cabbed it from the airport. I left before the conference closed. You didn't ask, but yes, my presentation went brilliantly."

"Didn't doubt it for a minute."

Roger tugged at my sleeve, steering us to a crowd surrounding Nico.

"How's the Jamaican doing on the case?"

"I was about to call Manny as soon as I got out of here. I don't think it's moving fast."

"I'd appreciate if we could call him together. Captain Falco gave me his silent blessing to poke my nose into the mess."

"*My* Captain warned me to stay far away," I said. "Personal conflict, I knew the victim, blah, blah, blah. You know the speech."

Roger smiled. "I guess we'll be working together with Manny then."

"Un-officially," I said.

I plowed into the crowd, Roger and his suitcase tagging along in my wake.

I forwarded Pat's condolences to Nico and Carmen.

"She's stuck in Quebec City and said she's mortified for not being here," I added.

I kissed Carmen on the cheek and whispered, "Call me if Nico or you need anything."

She nodded.

Roger touched the center of his forehead, feigned wiping his chin, and scratched his right earlobe before hugging Nico. More of their secret codes.

I deduced that Roger needed a lift when he followed me as I headed to my car.

I wiggled my fingers in front of my face. "What was that all about?"

"Told him I'm on it, we're working together, unofficially, and to call me later."

"You'll have to teach me those signs. It could come in handy someday."

"It's the non-verbal we Narcs use in undercover work. You, as a homicide cop, use nine-millimeter shots as your non-verbal."

"My reputation as a gunslinger is greatly exaggerated. Often, and venomously, by Internal Affairs." I said.

"I heard that Trehearne didn't pass his range test last month and he has to do another exam soon. Since you're such an expert marksman I think there's some negotiation currency available." Roger touched the center of his forehead.

"Interesting info, it may be of value."

"If you wipe an imaginary tear from your right eye, it means I see or heard and understand. Wiping the left of course, would be I don't," Roger said.

The lessons had begun.

In my Jeep, I brought Roger up to speed with what little I had so far. I added the info from Dobson on the twenty-two magnum rifle and the trail bike tire marks next to the car.

I put my phone on the console between Roger and I. Manny answered my call on the third ring.

"You free to talk?" I asked.

"Me okay."

"You're on speaker phone, and I'm with Detective Roger Lamont, Nico's partner.

He's got his chief's okay to help out anyway he can," I said diplomatically.

"Aright, a'm stuck on three other bad, bad, bad cases. I'm be fine with help."

"From what I've learnt," Roger said, "the murder wasn't planned, it was opportunistic, and it was someone that was known to Aldo as not dangerous. The fact that the air-conditioner noise hid the sound of approach was a pure coincidence due to the freak heat wave. The murderer wasn't worried about frightening his victim, nor the fact that Aldo may have been armed."

"I was leaning that direction," Manny said.

"The trail-bike tracks next to the car tell me the odds are that you are looking for a younger person, not someone older than forty," Roger said.

"What bike tracks?"

It was obvious that there were a few bumps in our inter-department information flow.

Roger profiled the killer for a few minutes more before Manny hung up with the promise to "Link up later."

On the drive to his apartment Roger said,

"You hungry? I think my meager airplane food has now reached my toes."

"I'm always hungry. I'm not averse to an early lunch. It'll give me the strength to endure another of Trehearne's sermons."

During our meal, Roger spoke of his Quantico psychology seminar and soon lost me in the clinical details of his presentation. Probably noting my second yawn, he suddenly stopped and asked about Pat. I spoke of Pat's frustration with the political aspects of her job with UPAC. He agreed with Pat's views on the political BS now gumming-up the Quebec justice system.,

By end of coffee-time, our bitching session was over, and Roger had that unfocused look of jet lag.

On my route for my convocation from ferret-faced Trehearne, I dropped Roger off at his mid-town apartment.

As I drove away, I mentally kicked myself for not telling him about my case with the Mascara Man. His profiling skills would have proved invaluable.

- 13 -

Trehearne's office layout hadn't changed from my last visit, months ago. He still had his medieval high-backed wooden visitor's bench. I scooped up the stack of papers littering the seat, slid the pile under his keyboard and straddled the chair.

"You should get rid of this monstrosity. The notch in the arm shows where the thumb screw was. And you still have dangerously tilting stacks of paperwork on your desk. You need a filing clerk and an interior decorator."

"A, there's a budget freeze, and B, this meeting isn't about housekeeping. It's about your usual heavy handed transgressions during arrest procedures."

"Heavy handed? Did you see the security tapes my boss sent you? Four guys jumped me."

"You didn't follow procedures. You didn't ask for back-up. If you had, there might not have been a fight."

"You have to get out from behind your piles and files, Lorne. Get back to the real world. We wasted three months hunting for Joseph Allen Brody. He'd disappeared into the woodwork."

"I know, I know, you managed to singlehandedly capture a wanted rapist and murderer, and your Captain always backs you up because you get results."

Trehearne stood up and perched on the edge of his desk, one hip askew and one leg dangling. It wasn't a pretty position, and it disturbed me. When he stood, it was usually a precursor to one of his pedantic speeches.

"It's not your results that we question, Beaudry, it's your methods."

"Polonius said, 'Though this be madness, yet there's method in it.' If you sit down, I'll explain."

Trehearne didn't budge from his perch. "I had a tip from a pizza delivery kid that *thought* he recognized Brody in an East-end pool hall. Not something solid enough to call out the riot squad.

Also, if you got out more, you'd know that back-up means patrol cars, noise, and attention from street look-outs. My quarry would have vanished faster than a downtown Saint Catherine Street parking space."

"Who's Polonius?"

"He's a Shakespeare character. It was just a line from a play. Relax and sit down, Lorne. You I.A. guys don't get it. I've been a detective for seventeen years. I know what I'm doing. The rule book doesn't catch criminals, leg-work does it."

"I've been on the job longer than you have, Beaudry. I've worked on the streets. Now my job is to make sure our officers are honest and follow the rules so as to not to compromise a conviction."

"Sit down, Lorne. Do we have a problem with the Brody arrest?"

"Nobody's complaining nor pressing charges, even with a list of broken fingers, a fractured clavicle, and one guy with four missing teeth and a dislocated jaw. I don't understand. I saw the tapes. You beat the stuffing out of them."

"They're bikers. They won't complain, they'll try to get even."

"Your disrespect of the rules will get you killed one of these days. Your James Bond-moves won't save you."

"Sit down, Lorne. Bond is old fashioned. Now it's Jason Statham."

"What is it with the sit down, sit down?"

I smiled a crooked smile. "Your crotch is at my eye level. I can see that you dress to the left. It's an observation I could have done without."

Trehearne started with a snicker that turned into contagious laughter. In a mere minute, years of tension between us dissipated. At the end of our outburst, we sat face to face, and for the first time we had an intelligent conversation.

He spoke of being ill at ease when his boss asked him to tap the phone of a local newspaper crime reporter who often knew the juicy facts of a case before the brass did. They wanted him tailed twenty-four/ seven to find who his police informants were. I commiserated and spoke of Pat's disappointment on the outcome of her UPAC investigations. We talked about office politics, and this and that.

Twenty minutes later, the niceties over, I was advised that the Brody file, as well as the recent gun play and wounding of Bosede Duff were both cleared by Internal Affairs. However, I did learn of something worrying. Lorne's off-the-cuff comment that *he* never had anything against me, and was glad that we finally had a heart-to-heart gave me the uneasy feeling that one of his higher–ups had me as his personal target. I didn't press the matter, nor did I volunteer my expertise in pistol training. It's always good to keep a spare card up your sleeve.

Before I left headquarters, I checked with Lorna, one of the Captain's clerical assistants. She said my boss was stuck in a meeting for at least another hour. I rushed to his office, wrote him a note saying that I was sorry I had missed him, and that I was now cleared by I.A.

During my escape to the parking lot, my phone rang, indicating 'unknown number'.

"You've reached Lieutenant Beaudry, talk to me."

"Good afternoon, Robert, this is Annick. I'm downtown and I'd like to invite you for a before-supper drink," she purred.

"This is a surprise. We haven't spoken in years. To what do I owe this sudden invitation?"

"I saw you at the funeral this morning. You look good. It's a shame we lost touch." In a whispered conspiratorial tone, Annick added, "I have to talk to you, it's important."

She gave me the name of a Mountain Street bar, asked me to meet her at five o'clock, and hung up.

- 14 -

I had time to let Crackers back into the apartment, feed him, hide the toilet paper roll, grab his new attack obsession—the fern from the living room—lock it in the bedroom, and make it on time for my tête-à-tête with Annick.

I found her in the last booth of the dimly lit bar. I didn't need any detective skills. Her low-cut orange dress was an attention-getting beacon. The side-glancing guys at the bar would have cricked necks tomorrow.

Annick had the eyes of an angel, but a wanton smile that would make a succubus proud. She stood and hugged me.

I said, "That's quite the dress you've painted on."

"It's so chivalrous of you to notice. If you've got it, flaunt it, has always been my motto."

"Well, everyone's noticed. I think that the businessman on the last stool is tilting precariously. He's about to fall over."

As she slid back into the booth, she showed a little more thigh than she needed, fluffed her hair, and winked at the hapless man.

I maintained my tough-guy reputation by pretending to ignore the show.

"What's the something important?"

"You haven't changed, Robert. Your police job always comes first."

Annick signaled the barman with two raised fingers.

"I'm sick over my brother's murder. The whole family is disturbed. It's incomprehensible to us why this happened."

"I didn't get a chance to offer my condolences to you this—"

"I don't need your condolences, Robert. I need you to find the *cazzo*."

The waiter brought an opened bottle of 2013 Marchesi Antinori Tignanello, and without asking, poured us each a glass. He tied a linen napkin to the neck of the bottle, turned, and rushed back to the bar as Annick raised her glass.

"In boca al lupo."

"I've never figured out what being in the jaw of a wolf has to do with wishing someone good luck," I said. "I'll take the luck, but I'm not on the case, Annick. My boss told me to butt out. I'm too close to the victim. I can't be involved."

"We know you're working unofficially. We'd like you to advise us, *unofficially,* of your progress."

"We?"

Annick's answer was a smile that belonged to someone who would never wear a halo.

"I appreciate the confidence that *we* have in my abilities, Annick, but the officer in charge of the case will make the arrest, if and when… I don't control that."

I took a sip of wine; it went down as smooth as a con man's patter, but her next sentence spoiled the enjoyment of the moment. It was evident that she had her sources and already knew too much inside information.

"The very laid-back Manny Agnant is spinning his wheels, and the theoretical Professor Lamont is not our first choice. You are. I could meet you anywhere, anytime." Annick dipped the tip of her tongue in her wine, and then licked her lips as she stared at mine.

"Pat has filled my date book, and I'm not looking for more work. I'm already overloaded." I rolled my eyes.

"Get off your high horse, Robert. We just want justice to be done."

"I'm pretty sure that somewhere in my job description there's a paragraph that includes preventing a homicide," I said. "I'm not always happy with a court's decision, but justice isn't cement boots and a plunge into the Saint Lawrence River."

"Don't get melodramatic. We're sure you'll find the killer. You always do. We just want a heads up before it goes public."

Annick gave me the full-wattage smile. I gulped my wine.

"We want to make sure Aldo's family is safe."

"Well, that's a point we can both agree on," I said.

I switched the conversation to small talk, and Annick diplomatically followed my lead. She described her new house and detailed her future decorating plans.

"I'm not keeping a stick of the old furniture. Everything will be modern. I've designed a new kitchen, with an integrated Gaggenau fridge and a wine climate cabinet. It'll be all new stainless appliances. Only the best."

"Sounds like an expensive project. Did your tough-looking boyfriend approve the dream-house budget? I'd hate to see you outlined in chalk on your new marble floor."

"Giovanni, he just looks mean. He's putty in my hands."

I didn't question the validity of her claim, nor the depth of her charms.

She left when the waiter disposed of the empty bottle. The guys at the bar glanced up in sequence as Annick slowly strutted by with a walk that was more Saturday night than Wednesday afternoon.

I had time to spare before my meeting with Antonio, and I figured I needed some energy to face the biker gang. My appetite awoken by the tasteful blend of Sangiovese and Cabernet, I ordered the mega smoked-meat platter.

When I asked the waiter for the damages, I wasn't too surprised to find the hundred-and-thirty-dollar wine added to my bill.

* * *

On the road to meet him, I called Antonio.

"I'm headed to the gym and I've attracted a tail," I said. "Two gorillas in a light-silver AMG Mercedes. Any suggestions?"

Michael Kent

- 15 -

I followed Antonio's instructions and motored past the gym, turned south on the next block, then west on a one-way side street. At the first turn, a flame-red dually pickup slid in behind me. On the second turn, a black van followed our little procession, surreptitiously boxing in the Mercedes. I continued down the road, as if unaware of the tails, turned north at the next intersection, and headed back to the gym.

When I walked into his office, Antonio was on the phone, chuckling about whatever the person on the other end of the line was saying.

He hung up as I sat in one of the overstuffed chairs across from his desk.

"What's the joke?"

"You missed a fender bender down the street. Must'a happened right behind you," Antonio said.

"Was a light-silver color Benz involved?"

"You must be psychic. Apparently, some superstitious truck driver slammed on his brakes because he saw a black cat crossing the street. The Merc plowed into the truck's rear bumper and tow-bar."

"Well, they do say that a black cat crossing your path is a bad omen. Nobody hurt, I hope."

Antonio pointed to the espresso machine on the credenza behind his desk. I nodded yes.

"A team of young basketball players stepped out from the van behind the accident. They volunteered to jump up and down on the hood of the Benz to help untangle the wedged bumpers."

"Very gentlemanly of them."

Antonio poured a cup and placed it close to me on a stained Canadian's cardboard coaster.

"It appears that in their enthusiasm, they left a few dents on the hood and front fenders."

"Can't blame them for trying to help."

"They did manage to free the cars and put the mangled bumper parts in the guy's trunk."

I took a sip; it was his usual dynamite strong blend.

"The Mercedes owner must have been relieved," I said.

"The Italian driver and his passenger didn't want the cops, or any hassles about insurance. They just wanted to get back on the road in a hurry."

"Italians?"

"Yes, the swear words gave them away. Two characters in expensive tailored suits, but that didn't quite conceal their armament," Antonio said.

"That may hint at their profession."

"What did you do to have gunsels following you?"

"I shared a bottle of wine with Annick DiLalla. Rumor has it that her boyfriend is a made-man."

It was the first time I saw Antonio smile. "*Cherchez la femme.*"

"Did your people get the license number?"

"The pickup driver insisted on a picture of the registration, just in case."

"You're going to leave me in suspense?"

For an instant, Antonio's dark eyes held a glint of amusement.

"The Mercedes is registered to a Miss Annick DiLalla."

"Rats, the bitch set me up."

Antonio's phone buzzed away the derogatory comment I was formulating in my mind.

Antonio looked at the phone's screen.

"I've had someone watching the pool hall since we spoke yesterday."

He listened for a few seconds and then hung up.

"The bikers have a management meeting to accept a new member. They'll be celebrating. A couple of cases of hard, and seven kegs were delivered this morning."

"We have another two hours before it gets really dark," I said. "I would have preferred an entrance under the cover of night. However, it would be best to face them before the drinking starts in earnest. I'd rather brave an enemy with a sober trigger finger than an armed drunk."

Antonio leapt out of his chair and opened the door to his storage room. "Let's get ready."

"Somebody's itching for action," I said.

He came back a minute later wearing an ankle-length black trench coat. He tossed me a soft body-armor vest. I pulled off my T-shirt and slipped on the Kevlar undershirt. While I dressed, I asked, "What's with the Keanu Reeves outfit? I hope you're not planning a Matrix lobby shoot-out."

"The right equipment for the right job."

He put his hands in his pockets and did a slow turn, as if modeling the raincoat.

"I had it custom made by a tailor I know."

Although his hands appeared to be resting in his pockets, in a blink, two double barreled pistol-grip coach guns flashed out of the raincoat, one in each hand.

Like the explanation of most magic tricks, his arrangement was deceptively simple. The shotguns were down along each side of his body, hung from a lanyard around his neck. The coat pockets had pass-through zippered bottoms, permitting him to have both hands on the weapons on the inside of his long jacket. Unless someone already had the drop, his draw would be the fastest, and with four twelve-gauge buckshot loads, very deadly at short range.

"Does your tailor double as a gunsmith?"

He doffed the coat and guns without an answer, draped everything on the back of his office chair, and sat down.

We went over the original plan that Antonio had formulated.

"Don't stand close to the plate glass window," he reminded me. "If there are gunshots, my friends the gang-bangers will drive the van into the window and come out shooting."

"I thought they were a basketball team."

"Whatever. Don't complain Robert, they'll be protecting your ass."

"No complaints, I'll follow your lead."

Antonio stood, wrapped his Keanu raincoat around the shotguns. Holding the bundle in the crook of his arm, he motioned me towards the office's emergency exit.

I emptied my weapon and followed Antonio out the back door to the alley and his Bimmer.

* * *

By the time we arrived at our destination, the sun had set and a pink southwest sky announced a potential bright day for tomorrow. I hoped I'd see it, and not from a hospital bed.

A familiar black van was parked two doors down from the biker's pool-hall-bar. Four Harley-based choppers framed the club's entrance, two on each side of the main entrance.

I strolled into the bar and took a position to the right of the entrance. Antonio sidled in a few feet next to me.

To our left, in an alcove, were the three pool tables where I'd had the run-in with a few of the gang members during my arrest of Allen Brody.

We faced the bar and six tables. Two of the tables were occupied: four patched members at one, and at the other, a sumo wrestler-sized guy, and, I presumed, the new recruit who had gone through the initiation ceremony. He had a bruised face, a very swollen lip, and, was handcuffed.

Mister Sumo blemished the Japanese clean faced tradition with a ZZ Top beard.

Vern 'Van Damme' Demers, the head honcho, sat on the bar facing his acolytes.

The room was silent, everyone staring at me as I held my locked open pistol at face level in one hand and my empty magazine in the other.

"I'm here to apologize for my enthusiasm of the other week, and to suggest collaboration on something of mutual interest."

One of the four guys seated at the farthest table had two of his fingers in a taped splint. He jumped up and reached under his shirt. I didn't recognize him. But then, everything happens real fast in a street fight, and I hadn't taken any selfies.

Antonio barked, "No," as one of his coach guns flipped out, and then back into to his raincoat. The movement was an impressive blur. "The lieutenant isn't armed, but I am. If you reach for a weapon, you die."

Everything froze in place. The biker with the splint on his fingers thought better of drawing his piece, and sat back down. I put my pistol on a nearby table but kept the empty magazine in my left hand.

The club's president Demers jumped off the bar and landed in a karate stance.

"You better have a good story, pig. I don't care about your short friend and his little shotgun. If I don't like what I hear, neither of you are walking out of here."

"That's a replay of what the boys told me when I arrested Brody, one of your hangarounds. By the way, I didn't have time to tell your guys that Brody is a rapist and a pedophile with a penchant for young boys. I'm not sure that they would have backed him up knowing that."

While I spoke, Demers stepped toward me.

"This is this just bullshit," he said to my face. His eyes reflected nothing, a look of total emptiness. I thought I might be in more trouble than I had bargained for.

He was fast; I had to give him credit. He feigned a kick and switched to a karate one-inch punch. I swiveled, but not quickly enough. His strike didn't hit my solar plexus as he intended; it grazed my left ribs and shoved me back a foot or so.

"Good shot Demers, but you only get one try."

I did a backhanded dismissal wave at Antonio who had stepped in, and now had the left shotgun in Demers' groin and the right one covering the members sitting at the tables.

Antonio shrugged, and glided three feet to the right. His move was as smooth as a dance step. The shotguns, seemingly magnetized to their aim-point, stayed right on target.

Demers totally ignored Antonio and his weapon. He turned abruptly, as if to walk back to the bar, but his movement blended into a spinning right-leg kick. This time I was prepared. I stepped outside the arc of his leg and, with my left hand still holding the empty pistol magazine, I hammer-fisted his ankle as his foot swung past.

As if nothing happened, I said, "I never bullshit, I'll pay you a coffee, and let you read Brody's file anytime. He wasn't a viable candidate. A pedo wouldn't be good publicity for the club."

I stuck my right hand out.

"Vern, let's shake on a temporary truce. And I'll explain where we can work together."

His lower lip was tight and his eyes narrowed. The sharp pain that I had inflicted was a game changer. He half tuned from me, no longer in an aggressive stance.

"I don't shake hands with a pi–cop. But I'll buy you a drink."

Demers forced himself to swagger back to the bar, his right foot slightly lagging behind. Antonio preceded him and went around to the service side, a good concealment zone, and a strategic position to cover the room.

A half bottle of scotch and a few beer chasers later, I had given Demers the basics of my plan. He addressed Antonio, who was now acting as the bartender.

"Is this guy a real detective?"

"Yeah, but he trusts street justice more than today's courts."

"I don't want to start another biker war," Demers said. "You don't need to kidnap Lamarsh. All you need is his phone—you can call the hired killer and track his cell. Bang, you got his location."

"I have no tangible justification, even if logic tells us the killer is working for The Rock Machine. They're the only ones that gain from the removal of the judge, the lawyer and witnesses against them. But the courts don't operate on intuition, or gut feelings, only provable facts."

Demers smiled, "Which means you're fucked without us."

Antonio was still pouring drinks. As the evening progressed, the atmosphere had become more jovial. Demers and I were at the bar, the rest of the gang playing drunk-man pool with the new recruit.

"I'd prefer having you on board, but I do have a plan B."

"Never mind your plan B, I think we can help each other. I wouldn't mind seeing that gang change address to Ste. Anne-Des-Plaines. It would open up new territories for us," said Demers.

"If we can tie them in to the hired killer they'll be guests at that maximum security hotel for many years," I said. "What about getting to Lamarsh?"

"Lamarsh is not a good enforcer. He's too vulnerable. His weaknesses are snorting and pussy," Demers said, with a noticeable slur on the last word.

"We all are men, in our own natures frail, and capable of our flesh; few are angels," I said.

To my astonishment, Demers asked, "Chaucer or Shakespeare?"

"The latter. You read the classics?"

"Don't judge a book by its cover. I have a BA in English lit. In this context I prefer Hubbard's 'Every saint has a bee in his halo.'"

"I'm duly impressed—motorcycles, literature and Karate, a wide range of interests."

Demers shrugged. "Wing Chun. You?"

"Mostly weights, some boxing, and Tai-Chi. But Antonio wants to teach me Krav Maga."

"Humm, cool. I can put Lamarsh out of action for a day and get you his phone. The best I can do without a war."

"I'll work with that. When?"

Demers clinked his shot glass against mine. "I need a day to get some out-of-town girls lined up. Gimme a number. I'll call you."

Both of us, typing slowly on strangely uncooperative virtual keyboards, exchanged our cell numbers.

* * *

We left, minutes past the witching hour.

Antonio hadn't touched a drop all evening. He insisted on driving me home, and told me he'd have someone leave my car on my street tomorrow morning. I didn't argue. The street lights and the passing scenery were pretty fuzzy.

Back at my place, I slopped Crackers's cat food in and around his bowl, then navigated to my bedroom holding onto the hallway wall. At the foot of my king-sized, I let go of a supportive dresser and half-undressed, let myself drop onto my mattress.

I had the cooperation of the bikers, but I was way out on a thin limb—procedure, and legal wise. I fell asleep ill at ease, as if I were driving toward a cliff edge with defective brakes.

- 16 -

I woke early. The low morning sunlight sneaking between the louvers of the bedroom window painted stripes across the rear wall. From my sideways lying perspective, the dark and light pattern reminded me of jailhouse bars, and of last night's bikers and their prison tats. The pain behind my eyes reminded me of last evening's drinking excess.

A tickle on my nose had brought me back from a dream. I expected it to be a wake-up tap from Crackers. I was stunned to find not a furry paw, but an errant curl from a redhead.

I woke Pat when I pulled my numbed arm from under her. She twist-turned to face me.

"Saints be praised. It's alive."

"I didn't hear you come in," I grumbled.

"Himself was boozed out and comatose. You would'na heard a lorry chug through the room."

"I don't remember anything. I'm so glad that you're here."

"Don't try your sweet-talk. What about last night's drunken groping and hugging me so tight I couldn't breathe?"

My face hurt. Nevertheless, I tried a smile.

"I can see that I have no pants or shirt, but I can't believe I'd stoop to drunken groping."

"I undressed you and tossed the sheet over your scuttered self. You were paralytic. Out tomcatting around were we?"

"No drunken groping?"

"That was just to add interest to my tale. You did hug the breath from me, though."

Pat rapped a heavy finger on my brow. It resounded in my brain as if my head was a bass drum.

"Your breath smells like the rear dock at the Guinness factory."

"No tomcatting. I negotiated a truce with the bikers from my bar fight of a couple weeks ago."

"Methinks the operative word here was *bar*," Pat said.

"Well, there may have been a few celebratory drinks involved. I'll make it up to you. I'll treat you to breakfast at your favorite French pastry place."

"That sounds tempting, but we're not going anyplace before you shave the stubble off your cheeky face and take a long shower."

I rolled out of my side of the bed and saluted. *"Oui, mon général."*

Pat was one surprise after another. She joined me in the shower where we shared some soapy slippery groping. Later, with satisfied and dreamy looks on our faces, both of us finally dressed.

* * *

The shower calisthenics opened our appetites and put us in the restaurant past the morning rush. We shared the venue with only a few dallying retirees.

"You've blueberry jam on your chin and I think you dropped some on your shirt," Pat said.

I dipped my paper napkin in my water glass and removed the offending spots.

"There's a big grin on your kisser. Are you laughing at my sloppy eating?"

"I'm happy today. Quitting that job has removed a weight from me. I feel twenty pounds lighter."

"Not if you eat that second pancake."

Pat slid her plate towards me. "You're eating like a ravenous wolf this morning."

"I think that you fed the ravenous wolf in the shower this morning," I said. "Too busy yesterday, I didn't eat much."

"Too busy downing the pints, were you?"

"I see I'm still on the hook for drunkenness."

With a two-inch right sided tilt of her head, Pat nodded. "Men forget but never forgive. Women forgive but never forget."

I changed the conversation. "I take it the meeting with your boss went well."

"Commissioner Martin was very sympathetic. No hard feelings, he praised my work and gave me a glowing recommendation. I'm back in the fraud squad with a promotion to team leader. And I don't report in till Monday."

"Wow, that's fantastic. Where are you based?"

"I'll be working from headquarters downtown, and sometimes on the road for captures."

"Just what you wanted, but the traffic from the West Island to headquarters every morning will be a pain."

"There's that, and, I was after telling you that I'd like to get rid of my house. There are too many bad memories of my ex there for me."

I took a sip of my orange juice and cleared my throat. "Pat, we've been together for a year. Maybe it's time we found a place together. I can easily rent my apartment in Old Montreal."

Pat dropped her fork onto the table, and her eyes glistened with tears.

"I guess that himself really did miss me."

I slid off my seat, went to sit on her side of the booth, and gave her a fast kiss. An old man sitting alone at a middle table raised his coffee cup to me in a salute.

She kissed me back but said, "Get back to your side, you big oaf. People are staring."

"Remember the homicidal manic we chased together? He had a really nice apartment."

"Are you daft?" Pat shivered. "Have you lost your mind in the whiskey? I'd never live in that place. There's probably a million ghosts lurking."

"No, no, no. I meant the mid-town area. Where there are big solid duplexes. Streets with oak trees along the sidewalks."

Pat made big round eyes at me. "Close to work, but close to posh Westmount, the houses must be a zillion dollars."

I ignored the Irish exaggeration.

"The cash from the sale of your house plus some money I inherited from my dad, no problem."

Pat's eyes were glowing.

"Do you have time to house shop?"

"Actually yes, I'm waiting for news on my hit-man, and all I have, *officially,* is a cold case file that your uncle dumped on me so I won't have time to put my nose into the Aldo murder."

We did a high five, and I went to the cash to pay Rolland the owner, while Pat powdered her nose.

"What's the bill for the elderly man at the middle table?" I asked him.

"Mister Kendall? He used to come in for breakfast with his wife. She died last month. Now he just has coffee."

"Treat him to breakfast. Tell him it's on the house. Add it to my tab."

"Never mind. It will be on the house. So is your bill. It was nice to see you kiss Pat. You made me remember my youth and Caroline. Just be careful on the streets, Lieutenant."

* * *

While we were walking back to my apartment, my phone played a jazz tune from my back pocket. I fished it out of my jeans. It showed Manny Agnant on the screen.

I answered with my usual, "Talk to me."

"Crawb up, we found a two-two rifle inna dumpster a couple blocks from Aldo's. You ready?"

"Hang on a second," I answered.

I made a pouty face at Pat,

"They found the rifle that killed Aldo a few blocks from his house. Manny wants me to join him."

"You don't need my permission to do what you have to do, Robert. I'll scout for houses and tell you what I found when you bring me out to supper tonight."

I blew Pat an air-kiss. "I got the message."

Manny gave me the location and I told him I'd be there in a half-hour.

- 17 -

The dumpster was behind a pet supply and kennel facility just east of *les Galeries d'Anjou* shopping complex. The building fronted the west service road of Route 25, the expressway heading to the South Shore tunnel. When I finally got there, Manny lay on the hood of a patrol car catching rays from the noon sun. The beat officers were trying to look busy by pacing back and forth along the police-do-not-cross tape strung at the entrance of the driveway. In addition, two technical officers sat in their *service d'identification* van, doors open while they ate a snack.

"Sorry guys," I yelled. "A Smart car wasn't smart enough to know that it was in the blind spot of a transport truck that was changing lanes. I spent twenty minutes on the exit ramp to the shopping center before they untangled the mess."

The forensic identification team left their seats, and still holding their munchies, walked to me.

One of them pointed to Manny with his thumb and a twist of the wrist.

"The big guy didn't want us to touch anything before you got here."

I read his I.D. pin.

"Thank you, Officer Saba. I like to look at evidence just as the criminal left it. It gives me insights into how he was thinking."

The other techie took a delicate bite of his muffin. Saba raised his eyes and commented with a shoulder shrug. Manny was humming a tune and still sitting on the hood of the patrol car.

As we approached the dumpster, officer Saba gave me a pair of nitrile gloves. As I stretched one over my right hand, it became a paler blue.

"I think I need a large," I said.

Saba did his shoulder shrug again. I guessed that the techies didn't carry a range of sizes in their van.

I peeked into the open chest-high container. A foot or so of rifle barrel was visible under a green lumpy garbage bag.

I glanced back to Manny, "Where's the person who found this?"

"Back inna store. You want?"

"Absolutely, can you get him please?"

A few minutes later, a lanky youth in torn jeans and wearing a Guns N' Roses tee-shirt peeked out from the back fire door of the store. With his foot, he pushed the handle of a broom partially out the door so that it couldn't swing back shut. I signaled him to me.

"You found the rifle?"

The kid looked at his sneakers and mumbled, "Yeah."

"What's your name?"

"Daniel Nault."

The kid looked sixteen or seventeen at most.

"You work here, Danny?"

"I hate that name. Everybody calls me 'Not'."

I mimed tying a knot, "Knot?"

"No. 'Not' like no, no way."

I suddenly felt my fortieth birthday sneaking up on me, and that today may be a long day.

"Okay, Not, can you walk me through how you found the rifle? Just explain it as if you're telling me about a movie or a concert you saw. Make me feel that I'm there myself."

He nodded rapidly. "I came out of the back door, pushed open the lid and swung the poop in."

He looked at me with a satisfied smile on his face.

"Poop?"

"Yeah, it's my summer job. I help feed the animals and I clean up the cages. I had a bag of hamster sawdust and stinky cat litter to throw into the dumpster."

"When did you see the rifle?"

"Only after I swung the bag over it. I turned back from waving to see it had burst open. The boss doesn't like it when that happens. It stinks up the container awful."

"Turned back, from waving?"

"I waved to Jimmylee."

"You weren't alone?"

"Yeah, Jimmylee was waving good bye from his mom's car."

"Is this another employee?"

"Naw, he's just a kid. A retard, he comes in a couple of days a week. He just stares at the rabbits or the guinea pigs. His mom is a friend of Victor's. She says it calms him down."

I swallowed my impatience and tried to keep my voice level before I asked, "You were here. Where was he?"

He pointed to the left corner of the parking lot.

"She parks in that spot. Jimmy was already in the car waiting for his mom. He was making motor noises with his mouth."

I contemplated shooting the kid in the leg, but there were too many witnesses, and it would probably slow the questioning even further.

The motor noises piqued my interest. I remembered Dobson talking about trail-bike tracks at the scene. I took a deep breath.

"Jimmylee was in the parking lot with a view of the container before you came out?"

"I guess. His mom came out a minute after me."

"Is Victor another employee?"

"He's the boss."

"Not, can you do me a favor? Ask your boss to meet me here."

While Not gave me his fractured story, the CSI technicians had taken multiple pictures of the dumpster and of its contents. Saba looked at me, question marks in his eyes.

"Go ahead," I said.

He lifted the garbage bag carefully off the rifle and laid it in the other corner of the bin. They took more pictures, carefully, and what seemed to me, with exaggerated composition. At the end of their artistic shoot, I gave them a 'wait-a-minute' finger signal and went to the left side of the container for a closer look at the weapon.

I spoke to the technical team while I made my observations.

"Remington, model five-ninety-seven, semi-automatic, in twenty-two magnum, magazine fed. An older model with the shoulder and cheek piece of the wood stock roughly cut off. No front sights, eight or nine inches of the barrel sawed off with visible hacksaw blade marks.

It's a sloppy fast job, not something that a prideful gang-banger would do. More like a teenager with no experience."

I pointed to the left access next to the building.

"The gun tosser came in on a motorbike from that side. His back was to the parked car behind the tree. He didn't see the kid sitting in it."

I walked back to the front of the container and mimed the action.

"He opened the bin lid with his left hand and flung the rifle with his right hand. Straight in, like a javelin throw, fast, and with strength. It hit the left container wall with enough force to chip the stock. There's a sliver of wood on a garbage bag next to the rifle. He departed either by the right side and back to the highway or from the exit behind your technical truck. Look for motorcycle tracks in the dust. We're looking for a well built husky teenager that rides a motocross type bike."

Officer Saba was looking at me with wide eyes and a slack jaw.

"Did anybody take notes?" I asked.

Saba's partner had finished his muffin and held up his cell phone.

"Got it on video."

"Good job."

As I spoke, a slim man wearing tan pants and a checkered shirt came strutting out the fire door.

Wavy brown hair with a tinge of grey in the side burns, a tan complexion, and a droopy mustache gave him the appearance of a poster cowboy.

I stuck my hand out to shake his.

"You Victor?"

He straightened his stance and puffed his chest out, ignoring my offered handshake.

"Yeah, you want to see me? I didn't find the gun. I don't know how I can help. I'm only the kid's boss. I've got nothing to do with this."

"Jimmylee was waiting in his mom's car parked next to that tree. He may have seen the guy who tossed the rifle in your bin. I need to talk to him."

"I can't call Hui-Ju. She's married."

I had used up what little patience God gave me, with Not. I stepped closer to Mister Cowboy.

"Victor, listen carefully. I'm Lieutenant Robert Beaudry. I'm working against time on an active homicide case. Your unhelpful attitude tempts me to toss you and your fancy cowboy boots into a cell on a charge of obstructing justice."

I lowered my voice, and moved in a foot from his nose. "I don't care if you're boffing his mother while her autistic kid is engrossed with watching the rabbits. Get on your phone and get her down here. I need to talk to that kid."

Cowboy Victor's neck turned a redder shade of tan. "Ah, er, she really doesn't want my number appearing on her phone. Ah, can, can, I give you her cell and you call her?"

I guess Victor had it good and didn't want to spoil things.

I looked into his eyes. His worried look appeared genuine.

"There's a book entitled 'Necessary Errors.' Somewhere in the pages of that novel, the author writes, 'Everyday life continues during a love affair.'"

I stepped back and pulled my phone out of my jacket.

"I'm not here to jam you up. I just need to talk to the kid."

Victor said, "Thank you," and gave me the phone number.

- 18 -

I agreed to meet Mrs. Lee and her boy, not at the pet shop, but at a quieter restaurant in the nearby shopping complex. Not only in deference to her delicate romantic situation, but because I was starving—it was way past my lunchtime.

I set up in a cozy back booth and texted a short summary of my observations on the found rifle to Manny, who had disappeared into the store during the work with the CSI team.

He texted me back with a picture of the puppy he had bought himself. Sexy Annick's comment about his laid-back attitude now seemed an understatement.

Ten minutes later, Mrs. Lee and her son walked up to the table. Jimmy was a big round boy and appeared to be in the pre-teen quartile, older than I had envisioned him from Not's comments. His mom was an oriental version of the raven-haired Annick. Hui-Ju's iridescent satin skin and her dark almond shaped eyes were her first attractive features. Her well-proportioned athletic body encased in a low-cut frilly lavender blouse and tight white jeans came in a close second.

She guided her son to the inner side of the booth, sat next to him, and then fished out of her large purse a coloring book and a big box of Prismacolor artist pencils.

He chose pink and went to work on finishing a very complex geometric design that featured mostly pastel shades.

As I touched his book, I said, "Jimmy you're a good artist. That drawing looks very difficult."

He recoiled as if I had Tased him.

Hui-Ju clasped my outstretched hand with surprising force and un-restraint.

"He's a high functioning autistic. You can't touch him or anything that he's holding, and he's wary of men in general."

With her hand glued on mine, I was tempted to comment, "But you're not."

She hung onto my big mitt as if it were a rope tossed to a careless explorer stuck waist deep in quicksand.

Something about her demeanor rang of fear, or of a deep apprehensiveness that I had often observed in victims that had suffered a severe beating or that had been tortured.

I shoved the thought to the back of my mind.

"I think that Jimmy saw someone toss a rifle into the dumpster behind the pet shop." I said. "I need to ask him what he observed while he was waiting for you in the car."

"He won't have to go to court if he saw the person, does he?"

"I can't promise anything. It'll depend on what other evidence we have. If the suspect's fingerprints are on the rifle, it would suffice to put him with the weapon. If not…" I made a sad face at her.

"I can't have any publicity." I felt her hand tighten on mine. "I just can't."

I jumped into the game and squeezed back.

"I'll do my best to keep both of you incognito. That, I can promise."

Her tension subsided, her shoulders dropped an inch or so, and her arm and hand relaxed.

"He won't answer questions from a man. What do you need to know?"

"I think he saw a young man on a motorcycle toss a rifle into the dumpster."

She tugged at Jimmy's sleeve. He didn't look at her, but his pencil froze in mid-air, as he suddenly stopped coloring.

"Qîn'ài de, did you see a nice motor bike this morning?"

Jimmy flipped to a blank page at the end of his book, changed to a black pencil, and started a free hand drawing while making motor noises with his mouth.

As if she had suddenly awoken, Hui-Ju stared at her hand clamped over mine and gently released me.

"His drawings are very good. If there is something missing, I can ask him more questions."

"Are you hungry?" I asked. "I haven't had lunch yet."

"I'll share something with Jimmy. He likes to pick at my food."

* * *

By the time our plates were empty, I had Hui-Ju's back-story from Taipei, and learned about her ex-husband's terminal cancer, and her recent marriage to a wealthy owner of several veterinary clinics.

During our conversation, Jimmy had sketched a red bike complete with KTM logo and 1290 as the type. He also had the helmeted rider sitting astride. The view was in partial profile.

I could discern the mouth, jaw line, and cheeks of the clean shaved cyclist. He appeared young. His drawing wasn't good—it was as excellent as a snapshot.

He let his mom turn the coloring book toward me and I took a couple of pictures of his rendering. Jimmy was still making motor noises and slowly rocking forward and back.

"This is going to be a great help. Thank you."

"Jimmy remembers everything he sees, down to small details."

"Speaking of details, the bike's license plate is blank. Can you ask him about that?"

She didn't ask her son the question. She tapped the rear of the bike in the picture.

Jimmy started another drawing.

My next question was a shot-in-the-dark. But, her tight lips when she answered showed that I wasn't far from the target.

"You have several small bruises on both of your arms." I said. "Is there an abusive husband or lover you'd like to talk to me about?"

"It's complicated. We may talk in a week or so."

Her eyes and mouth morphed into a sudden look of distaste. I wasn't sure if she was thinking of her problems, or if my charm had fizzed out like last night's opened and forgotten can of beer.

Jimmy finished his close-up of the rear fender. It showed a paper or cardboard taped to the license plate. I took another picture.

Hui-Ju scooped up the book and pencils and signaled the waitress. As soon as the tab hit the table, she grabbed it. From her deep purse, she peeled off a few bills from a fat roll of cash, dropped them on the table and stood up.

"I owe you one," I said.

"Keep us out of publicity Robert, and we're even."

I gave her my card. "If you need to call me."

She nodded and walked to the exit like a runway model, Jimmy skipping happily along next to her. I have to admit that I took a minute to appreciate the view of her departure. I took another minute to follow her to the exit and jot down the license plate of her white Audi Q5.

- 19 -

When I got back to my car, beige and white splotches decorated part of the roof and the rear passenger window. Some mischievous downtown pigeon had target practiced on my Jeep. Maybe the saying that it was a sign of impending good luck was true. On the downside, I knew it wasn't good for my paint.

My plan was to call Nico with the current news, then head to the car wash and home. He answered on the second ring with an out-of-breath rhythm to his speech.

"Hi Robert, you…were on my growing list of people to call…before my flight.

"I've left Manny and the tech team," I said. "I think we found the rifle that killed your cousin."

"I'd really like an update Robert. I'm completely out of the loop."

"I'll tell you everything I know."

"I can't use the phone. I'm waiting for the Italian consulate to call me back. I've had *molto* problems with the paperwork. I'm in a rush to get back to the airport. I'll be there until my flight."

"When's your flight?"

"Six fifty-five. Lufthansa sixty-seven, zero, seven."

"I'll meet you at Trudeau," I said.

I hung up and speed-dialed Pat.

"I was about to call you," she answered.

"I have to meet Nico at the airport before his flight. You okay with a late supper?"

"All right by me. I have great news. Meet me at my house. I'll swing by and pick up Crackers."

"Great news?"

She hung up after saying, "Savage it is. See you later."

My heart belongs to her, but we had never lived together in the same space week after week. I enjoy her teasing me when she's in a frilly nightgown, but today's 'savage news' banter had me a bit worried. Not that I had qualms about my impulsive statement to her of 'let's get a house together,' but...

Metropolitan expressway wasn't living up to its name. The lanes were crammed with sluggish and halting traffic. I asked myself, where were all these drivers coming from at ten to three in the afternoon? What happened to a nine-to-five workday?

Condemned to follow the molasses flow of cars, I used the time to call the Captain's administrative assistant, Janet. Like a happy face Emoji, she had a perpetual smile, and a constant cheery outlook. In O'Neil's sourpuss office, she deserved a medal.

"Hellooo, Lieutenant. To what do I owe the honor of your call?"

"I need a quick favor, and yes I do owe you a lunch for the last favor. Not forgotten, Janet, just delayed."

"Not to worry, I know the boss has you hopping. The office is abuzz with the news of you solving the *burnt girl* case."

"The credit should be given to Tristan from the lab. He mocked up a composite of the girl's face. That's what gave me the break to solve the case."

"So handsome, strong, and humble."

"You're the only one in the office who appreciates my full valor," I said.

"Ask away, humble sir. What do you need?"

"I just texted you a license number. I need the owner's name and address."

"It could take a few minutes. Do you want me to call you back?"

"I'm stuck in traffic. Put me on hold."

"I read impatience in your tone. Hang on."

By the time I managed to cut into the faster moving left lane, Janet had the info.

"A white Audi four by four, registered to Jarcon clinics in Longeuil. The company has four other cars in its fleet. A Mercedes Sprinter, a Tesla, a Ford F three-fifty and a Lamborghini for dessert."

"Text me the details and the home address of the president of Jarcon."

"Yes master."

"Please, and thank you. Your choice of lunch restaurant," I said.

* * *

I had to leave my weapon in the airport security office. My credentials got me a pass to the Lufthansa gate area, but only with a young RCMP officer as my guide.

"Lufthansa's gates are at the end of Terminal B," she said. "A thirty-five-minute walk. Do we need a cart?"

"Naw, don't think so. I can carry you if you feel tired."

She gave me a crooked grin and took off at a trot.

Her name-tag was S. Lachance. I wondered if the S was for snarky.

By the time we arrived at gate 63 she had a few damp strands at the edge of her uniform cap, and I hadn't yet broken a sweat.

"You think you can find your way back?" Lachance said.

"Yah, I'm okay. I enjoyed your company but I'm sure you have better things to do."

She saluted smartly and took off as if chasing an escaped prisoner.

I turned and found Nico standing behind me. He rolled his carry-on closer to us and pulled a flower-print carpetbag next to it. "You flirting with a cute RCMP officer?"

"She was a big help through the security checks and paperwork, but not much of a conversationalist."

"Don't talk to me about paperwork. The Quebec and Italian *funzionarios* were in a contest to see who could bury us in red tape the deepest."

"How's Vanessa holding up?"

"*Non c'e male.* In the ladies', touching up her makeup, again."

Nico pointed to an empty bench. "*Prego.*"

I fished out my phone as we sat.

"We found the twenty-two in a waste container behind a pet shop a few blocks from Aldo's street."

"I know O'Neil wants you far from this," Nico said. "I was counting on Roger to keep me informed, but he's stuck negotiating a hostage situation."

"Don't worry about my boss. I never do."

I scrolled to the last pictures in my phone. "This is the man that hid the rifle."

"I don't recognize him. Looks like a kid." Nico raised his hands to heaven. "Why would he shoot Aldo?"

"I don't know yet. He could be a disgruntled busboy that worked in one of his restaurants. Could be he just tried to get rid of it for a friend. We'll find him. Manny's interviewed the restaurant staff and is now working Aldo's business contacts."

Nico slapped his brow. "Ma, no real clues yet."

"My gut tells me this picture will break the case," I said.

"My gut tells me I better eat before I get on the plane. I can't cope with the crap they now serve. *Ho fame*, I haven't had a bite all day."

Vanessa entered the gate waiting area, her head hung low. She wore an ankle length form-fitting black dress, decorated with see-through black embroidery around her neck and shoulders. She held a little black pork-pie hat, an attached veil dangling from it. With her purple lipstick and eye shadow, she looked more like a modern version of a witch than a grieving widow. People turned to look as she walked slowly to us.

"*Ancora non ci credo*,"

I stood and took her free hand. "I have difficulty believing it myself."

I pointed to my vacant seat. "No, I'll be sitting for hours in the plane," she said.

From my phone, I showed her the picture that Jimmy had drawn. "Do you recognize this man?"

"No. Does this have anything to do with my Aldo?"

"Just a potential witness."

"Can't see his face very well with the helmet. I don't remember seeing anyone resembling that."

She took the phone from my hand and stared at intently at the sketch. "I remember picking up Adrianna at school, months ago. She was talking to a young man on a motorcycle similar to this, but *arancione*."

"A bike like this, but orange?"

"I think so. I just glanced at it."

The gate attendant announced pre-boarding. Aldo stood up and waved to me as he headed to a food stand. "Text me."

I kissed Vanessa on the cheek and wished her good courage.

I made my way back to security to collect my weapon. I was uneasy, as if I had something on the tip of my tongue but was unable to recall it or to give it shape.

Michael Kent

- 20 -

I paid the exorbitant airport-parking fee and collected my Jeep from the valet.

"For that price, you guys should have parked it, and washed it."

"They have a new econo-parking, seventeen bucks, including a free shuttle. Thirty minutes to the departure lounge."

"I know. I was in a rush to meet someone. Sorry, just venting for nothing."

He smiled and handed me my key fob, leaving his hand out. "Don't forget the tip," he said.

I called Pat as soon as I started the car. "I'm just leaving the airport. I can pick you up in about twenty minutes."

"I'd like to eat in for a change. I've volunteered you as chef for tonight, but I'll take care of dessert."

"Okay, I'll pick up the makings. So, what is this great news?"

"We'll talk over supper. Sorry, I have to let you go. I have someone at the door."

Often when your girlfriend opens with 'we have to talk,' it's generally not good news. With Pat, I was not too worried, but very curious.

* * *

After a quick stop at the *Marché de L'Ouest*, I installed myself in Pat's kitchen.

"Baked almond crusted chicken breast, caramelized baby carrots with grilled red bliss potatoes, is our menu today. If *madame* can open a bottle of wine, we can talk while I play *ze* chef."

"Red or white?"

"I saw a bottle of La Crema Chardonnay in your rack. That would be fine."

Pat was humming to herself while fighting with the corkscrew.

"You're in a good mood. Share it with me while I prep."

Pat winked at me, "Luck of the Irish."

She managed the cork and poured me a taste sample.

"I scouted streets in NDG taking notes on houses for sale, from Cavendish Boulevard toward Victoria. A few streets from Westmount, I came up a one-way to see Isabelle hammering in a For Sale sign into the lawn."

I nodded approval of the wine and held out my glass.

"Isabelle?"

"Fotopoulos, the real estate agent. I parked my car in the driveway and introduced myself. We talked and talked, like old friends, it was magic."

"I'm not surprised. You can charm the pants off anybody when you want."

"That'll be dessert. Let me finish my story." Pat topped my glass and poured hers. "Mister Roshefort, a retired dentist, is selling the duplex because his wife is hospitalized with an inoperable cancer. We met him, I visited his flat and the rental above, and I made him an offer."

"Whoa horsey. You made him an offer?"

"Isabelle said his asking price is low because he wants a fast sale, doesn't want to burden his kids, and he wants to spend all the time he can with his wife in the private care facility he booked."

I took a gulp of my wine. "I thought we were in this together."

"Well I want to talk to you about that."

I took another gulp, "Aww, rats, this doesn't sound good."

"Don't get your knickers in a knot. You've dropped egg shell in your mix."

I picked out the offending pieces. As she spoke, I whisked the eggs, dipped the chicken breast in the mix, then into a spiced breadcrumb mixture.

"You know I'm gone in the head about you. But I was under the thumb of my ex for a long time. I'm enjoying being in charge of my life. Yes, I want us to live together, but this is a deal I need to do for myself."

"I can understand, but it would have been nice to participate. And, what about the money?"

"You just missed Isabelle. She came to give me a market value for my house. With the figure she gave me, and the rental, I'll cover the small mortgage and make a few bucks every month."

"Irish luck, and good timing. I still feel left out, but happy for you." I clinked my glass against hers.

"You're not left out. The house is in good shape but he rents the top floor and lives downstairs. I want to do the contrary. They haven't renovated neither, nor painted in at least twenty years. I need a handsome, strong, and skilled woodworker to help me on the renovations."

"I knew there was a catch somewhere."

I wiped the excess breadcrumbs, re-dipped in the egg mix and coated the chicken thoroughly with almonds.

Pat made googly eyes at me. "In addition to free room and board, I can pay you in sexual favors."

"Well that sounds reasonable to me."

During our supper, Pat complimented me on a tasty meal and explained the details of the deal she'd made with her newfound friend Isabelle the real estate broker.

After coffee, Pat suggested a special dessert. I considered it as a down payment on my renovation contract.

Michael Kent

- 21 -

Pat had the comforter pulled up to her nose, sleeping with disheveled curls and a satisfied grin. After a trip to the washroom, I slid on jeans and tee shirt before investigating the thumping sound coming from the kitchen.

Crackers was rubbing himself against the screen of the sliding door, the present of a mangled chipmunk in his maw.

I traded his gift for a plate of his wet fishy-smelling treats and topped up his bowl of dry food. I wrapped his victim in a paper towel and laid it to rest, hidden in the compost bin outside. Pat had no hesitation at drilling nine-millimeter holes into a bad-guy, but was aghast when Crackers massacred anything furry or feathery.

I lived the Boy Scout motto: *Be prepared.* Yesterday, I had purchased foodstuff for supper, as well as the makings of next morning's breakfast. While Pat continued her delicate snoring, I prepared blueberry waffles, scrambled eggs, and a side dish of mixed fruit with English cream.

In retrospect, I was delighted with her decision to buy the duplex. Her years of marriage to that manipulative sleazy lawyer had whittled away at her self-confidence. Pat's decision to divorce the bum had been the first step in regaining control over her life. I couldn't argue with her therapeutic decision to buy her own home. I also agreed with an unknown writer that penned, "Love means partnership, not ownership, appreciation, not possession."

I spoiled Pat with breakfast in bed. She spoiled me back when she joined me in the shower.

An hour and a half later, I found my phone on the carpet, where Crackers had scored a goal by pushing it between the legs of the coffee table.

The screen indicated two missed calls, a voicemail, and a text that read, "URGENT-URGENT-URGENT- Take your messages."

I complied with the request. The voicemail was from RCMP Inspector Henschel.

"The Laverdeer passport came up on our system as used for I.D. yesterday noon at the Best Western Suites on Sherbrooke Street West. I can't send anyone. All our agents are protecting visiting dignitaries at a financial meeting in Ottawa. Get your butt to the hotel. I'll send you some modified pictures. Call me."

I thumbed the callback icon. Derek's answer was instantaneous.

"Where the frig are you, Beaudry?"

"Living my life. You should try it sometime."

"Are you on this, or not?"

"Yeah, yeah. Calm down," I said. "He's still using the *Laverdière* cover. It doesn't make sense."

"The French police haven't divulged the murder of the notary. The Mascara Man doesn't know the body's been found."

"The guy's a renowned international hit-man and a master of disguise. He should be someone else by now. I'm leaving for downtown now, but I have doubts about your info."

Derek hung up after another instruction, "Call me when you get to the hotel."

I told Pat about my conversation as I donned a sport shirt and a jacket to hide my shoulder rig.

She gave me a slap on the butt and told me to be careful.

* * *

The hotel's reception was manned by a smiling wide-shouldered, balding man and a snotty looking skinny guy with a toned down mullet haircut.

"Bonjour, does Monsieur 'ave a reservazion?"

I ignored the mock-Parisian and badged the big guy. "I'd like to know if this man checked in to the hotel. He'd be under Pierre Laverdière." From my phone, I showed him Derek's first picture of the Mascara Man.

He typed in the name and punched in a few more commands on his keyboard. "I have him as checked in, but—he never used his card-key. Hang on a sec." He went to the end of the counter and picked up a two-way radio.

The "Parisian" dropped the accent and moved closer to peek at the picture on my phone.

"I was on duty yesterday morning. I suspected something. He had no luggage and he specifically asked for a room on the sixth floor facing Sherbrooke Street and then asked for directions to the closest book store."

"You found that suspicious?"

"Not something our patrons do. There's too much construction noise on that side. Young couples don't seem to mind, but this guy was pretending to be in his late sixties."

"Pretending?"

"His neck appeared younger than his face. I think he was made-up to look older."

I read his name badge. "You don't miss much, François."

"I'm studying to be an actor. His make-up was very professional."

Smiley-Man came back to us. "I paged housekeeping. The room was never slept in."

I leaned closer to both of them. "This is a very discreet investigation. You can't tell anyone. Not even your boss."

"What's he wanted for?" asked Smiley.

"He's a witness in a murder case. It could be dangerous. A killer may be hunting him. He's afraid to testify in court and he skipped out on us," I lied.

François flashed me a plastic pass-key card. "The killer may be waiting in ambush. Do you want to check out the room with me?"

"Kid, your accent may be fake," I said. "But your balls are real."

Housekeeping was correct—the room appeared unused.

François said, "He's booked for a three day stay, early check out on Monday. He paid in advance."

"You said he asked for a bookstore. Where did you send him?"

"Indigo, on McGill."

I reminded François about keeping mum and gave him my card with instructions to call if Laverdière showed, or if anyone asked for him. I texted Derek with the news and headed for the street.

* * *

Indigo was doing brisk business that day. There was a ten-person lineup at the cashiers. I didn't want to create a fuss, so I walked back to the young greeting man at the store entrance.

I did my badge flip and asked to see his boss. Without a word or a question, he led me directly to her office.

The store manager—a pert, casually dressed shorthaired brunette—was affable and easygoing. I gave her the same song and dance I'd used at the hotel. After mere minutes, we were besties.

"I've read a lot of mysteries, but this is the first time I've met a real detective. I'll help you anyway I can."

"Much appreciated Debora, but as I mentioned, it's imperative that my scared witness doesn't know we're closing in on him."

"I wouldn't threaten easy. If ever I'm a witness to a crime, or if I'm chosen for jury duty, I'd not hesitate in doing the right thing."

"Good. I'd need to interview your floor staff to see if they served this customer. He's an actor, so he may be disguised."

From my phone, I showed her Laverdière's picture as well as the RCMP mock-ups of the Mascara Man with different hairstyles and facial hair.

"It's hard to see on a small screen. I'll give you our Wi-Fi code and you can print them full size here," she said.

She helped me send the seven pictures of the Mascara Man to the store server. She printed them on the Hp behind her desk.

To maintain discretion, she called each of her staff one by one to look at the rogues' gallery spread on her desk.

By the ninth person, it was clear that despite our requests for secrecy, the telephone game had spread twisted rumors through the store.

"Is this about the rapist the police are looking for?"

"No Katelyn, the Lieutenant is looking for a witness to a crime. No rapist, no axe murderer."

"Have you served this man?" I pointed to the row of pictures. "We think he may have changed his appearance. Please look at the composites carefully."

"I haven't seen him in the store. But I've seen *him* in the street." Katelyn put a finger on the black haired and mustached composite.

I stood up. "Him? On the street, where?"

"Coming out of the hotel. They have a five-dollar breakfast before eight."

"This morning at the Best Western?"

"No, no, breakfast at the Omni across the street."

I picked up the picture, "Katelyn, you're sure this is him?"

"Yes but his mustache is smaller, trimmed like Hitler and he wasn't wearing glasses."

I thanked Katelyn and left another card with Debora, who promised to check the rest of her staff and call me if anything else came up.

My call to Derek went to voicemail. "You were right, buddy. He changed hotels. He's at the Omni on the south side. I'm on my way.

I rushed to Sherbrooke Street, a sour taste of adrenaline in my throat.

- 22 -

I was at a standstill, jammed at the corner of Mansfield and Sherbrooke Streets. The intersection was car and pedestrian gridlocked, as a crane lowered a prefab manhole into a truck sized crater on the North side of the road. An officer in camouflage pants held the remote for the red traffic light that seemed painted on. Willing the light to green wasn't working.

My inoperative focus changed when I heard my name called from somewhere behind me. I turned to see ferret-faced Trehearne waving at me from the middle of a group of waiting pedestrians.

He yelled, "Wait for me," as the light changed and the crowd flowed around me.

"What are you doing here, Beaudry?"

"Chasing a suspect. What are you doing outside of your medieval office? I thought you were allergic to fresh air."

"Dropped off my daughter at the University. Chasing what suspect?"

"A hired killer. I had a tip he's holed out in a hotel down the street. And you've made me miss the light."

"A killer? Where's your back-up?"

"Under my left armpit."

"Your bravado attitude is what gets you in trouble, Robert."

"Relax. It's just a tip, not a certainty. If he sees a uniform he'll vanish like a fart in a hurricane."

"The only hurricane around here is you, Beaudry. I'm not in uniform. I'll be your back-up."

Trehearne had the anxious look of a puppy waiting for a bacon treat. "Well, ah, er. Don't screw this up, Lorne. Move your butt, the light's changed."

* * *

Lorne stood on tiptoes to peek over my shoulder when I showed my print of the dark haired, mustached version of the Mascara Man to the Omni desk clerk.

"His mustache is trimmed square like Hitler," I said.

"I don't recognize the face. I need his name to search the system."

"If I had a name I'd have given it to you. We need to interview your staff. This is an important witness in a murder case."

Trehearne tugged my sleeve, a frown on his face. "We don't want to panic anyone," I added. "But we need his testimony to make sure an innocent man doesn't wind up in jail."

Trehearne nodded comprehension, looked at his watch, then at James the desk clerk. "It's close to lunch time."

"I know, I'm starving," I said.

Trehearne overlooked my comment and continued with James, "Do your people eat in a staff cafeteria?"

"Yes, behind the restaurant kitchen. They'll be on their break in ten minutes."

James reached under the counter and handed me two plastic cards. "Lunch on the house."

Lorne took the picture from the counter and studied it. As if mesmerized by the face of the Mascara Man, he turned slowly, and still staring at it, walked away.

"Pick up some food, Beaudry. A club sandwich for me is okay. I'll wait in the employee cafeteria."

Ignoring the little gilded framed sign, I didn't wait to be seated. I found myself an empty table at the rear of the restaurant.

"Sorry, we don't do club sandwiches," my waiter said. "We have a chicken, bacon, and veggie wrap, or ham and turkey on French baguette."

I didn't overspend on his free meal voucher; I chose the French sandwiches and small salads to go, for both of us.

Situational awareness is probably the most important skill for staying alive in a dangerous world, and an essential asset at all times for a police officer.

I surveyed my environment and the restaurant patrons, thinking to myself, Mascara Man could be dining at one of these tables.

Pat would have credited some Irish magic, or the intervention of a friendly leprechaun, for as I soon as I formulated my thought, I saw my quarry pass the restaurant entrance as he headed toward the lobby.

I jumped out of my chair and ran to the restaurant exit, the dumbfounded waiter behind me, yelling, "Sir, Sir, your order."

I reached the lobby in time to see a glimpse of the Mascara Man wearing a dark blue blazer and tan pants before the doors swished close and the up-arrow lit.

My frustrated rush to the bank of elevators was for naught. All I could do was watch the floor numbers as they indicated the stops on the trip up.

It appeared as a milk run, the digital numbers reading halts at 3-4-5-6-7-8-10-11-12. Some smartass must have pressed rows of buttons as a dumb farce.

Disgusted, I fast-walked in the direction of the restaurant.

Nearly bowling me over, Trehearne came running out of a service door adjacent to the restaurant entrance, his badge hanging from a lanyard and flapping at each step.

"You run like a girl, Lorne."

"I got two hits. Room six-one-one-four."

We both rushed to a filling elevator.

"He went up a minute ago," I said. "I missed him by milliseconds."

As if in charge, Trehearne held up his badge and shooed everyone out of the elevator, barking, "Police business, police business."

He was taking his back-up role a little too seriously.

At the sixth floor, the elevator opened to a small alcove. Trehearne said, "Hold the door, Beaudry."

He rushed out, stole a flower pot from its perch in the corner, and jammed it in the door slot to keep the elevator held on our floor.

"In what movie did you learn that?"

Looking for the direction of the room numbers, he stepped around the corner and jumped back to hide at the edge of the wall, his eyes wide and his faced flushed. "It's on the left."

I had created a monster. I stepped in front of him.

"Cover the right side and my back."

We went around another bend in the hallway. Forty feet ahead of us, the Mascara Man was swiping his key-card at his door. He glanced at us, hesitated for an instant, flung the door open, and bounded into his room.

I pulled out my weapon and held it down along my leg. "We spooked him," I said. "He saw the badge around your neck."

"We have him cornered like a rat. I'll call for more back—" Before Trehearne finished his sentence, Mascara Man jumped out with a silenced pistol and put two rounds in the wall, inches ahead of me. His weapon still trained in our direction, he fired once more as he skipped sideways toward a stair exit across the hall, four doors behind him.

At the first pops of his pistol, I had dropped to the floor. I aimed and fired. In the same instant, Trehearne, standing to my right and behind me, in a bad imitation of a Weaver stance, emptied half of his magazine in the general direction of our shooter.

During the fray, the Mascara Man bent from the waist and grunted as a spray of blood patterned the wall next to him. He took two last shots at Trehearne as he went out of the exit. My ears ringing from the hellfire Trehearne had unleashed, I turned to see him unconscious on the floor behind me, white faced, eyes closed, lying on his right side.

I ignored my escaping felon and dashed to Lorne.

His pant legs were damp, from crotch to ankle, the blue fabric turning to a darker shade. I rolled him to his back, loosened his belt, tie, and popped his collar button.

I shook him, "Lorne where are you hit?"

He gasped a lungful of air, as he tried to focus his eyes, "My left leg is on fire."

I pulled out my penknife and slit his pant leg. He had two small caliber entrance wounds six or seven inches above his knee. He moaned and nearly passed out again as I tilted him on his side. I cut off his pant leg and tossed it aside. I was worried he was bleeding from an artery because of the light red blood color. He had two exit wounds at the back of his thigh. What was oozing out of the quarter-sized craters was darker, only turning pink as is flowed down his leg.

"I think I peed myself."

"Not important. The bullets went right through, didn't hit anything serious."

"You let him escape," he moaned.

"Never leave a wounded buddy on the battlefield. Anyhow, he's not going far. I think we put a couple on target."

"Oh my God, it's the first time I've ever taken a shot at another human being."

I used his pocket-handkerchief, tissues from a pack I always carry, and his tie, to compress the exit wounds. I didn't mention that he must have pulled the trigger in panic at least a half dozen times.

I phoned in the shooting and put out an apprehend request with a new description of the Mascara Man. All the area hospitals and clinics would be on the lookout.

While we waited for the *Urgences Santé* ambulance, I said, "At least, this time I'll have an easy interview with internal affairs."

As a team of first- responder firefighters came rushing toward us, Lorne gave me a lopsided smile.

"I now understand how fast shit happens on the street. It's a painful lesson."

- 23 -

An hour and twenty-five minutes after the shoot-out, uniformed officers were holding back reporters and downtown paparazzi from the sixth floor, and I was hosting a meet-and-greet in the hallway in front of the Mascara Man's room.

I had phoned my Captain and given him the highlights of my latest misadventure. He was now on the scene with a technical team. The Provincial Police delegated a couple of well groomed and near parade-perfect uniformed senior investigators—our Federal Government represented by a couple of nondescript spooks from the Canadian Security Intelligence Service.

Everyone wanted to hear my story, and then study the Mascara Man's room and his belongings.

The hotel manager, who until now, had been outstandingly cooperative and helpful, was still smiling, but with less enthusiasm.

"Tell the press you have a couple of incognito Hollywood guests, and they have police protection to stay that way," I said.

He headed back to reception after saying, "I think that story will make the situation worse. I'm going with an emergency preparedness drill, and leaving it at that."

The tech people finished their exam and photo-shoot of the room. With a warning about the finger print dust everywhere, they finally told us we could enter, but not to handle any of the marked evidence.

As usual, attention centered on Captain O'Neil. At six foot six and with the presence of an army general inspecting new recruits, he always took charge of any situation that he was called to.

He stood in the middle of the room, put his phone back into his jacket, and pointed to Jonah, the plump and balding headman from the tech team, and then to a spot on the floor in front of himself. Jonah stumbled with a nervous gait to his assigned location in the circle forming around the Captain.

O'Neil repeated his 'come here now' signal to most of us.

"Trehearne is in emergency, stable, and no serious damage. Beaudry, run through the event and explain why the hell Internal Affairs was on the scene of one of your shoot-em-ups– before the fact."

Using MM as an abbreviation for the Mascara Man, I did an edited version of my morning, and of the fortuitous meeting with Trehearne, up to the shoot out.

"He jumped out of his room with a suppressed weapon, pumped two shots at me. I dropped to the floor and shot at him twice. At the same time, Lorne sent five or six rounds in his direction. I hit MM at least once. It didn't stop him. He fled to the stair exit, and I took care of Trehearne."

"It sounds so simple and random when you tell it, Beaudry. I'm going to need a much more detailed written report, understood?"

"I'd expect so."

The Captain turned to Jonah. "Corroboration?"

The crime scene technician nodded, "Five three-eighty shells on the East side of the hallway. Two bullets in the North wall, we're still looking for the other rounds. Hard to find in the carpet design."

"Get more people. The hotel management wants the sixth floor back in business ASAP, and I want back-up on everything," O'Neil said.

The tech continued, "Two shells from the Lieutenant's side, we're hanging on to his weapon for a ballistics match. Seven shells from Sergeant Trehearne's weapon, also held for testing, the spent casings add up with what's left in both of their magazines."

One of the CSIS agents had a miniature recorder in his hand. The Provincial team were attentive, but would surely wait for the written report to hit their desk.

"What else?" Jean asked.

"From the bullet holes in the wall and floor, blood spatter and footprints down the stairs, I'd say the suspect was hit twice in the abdomen and once in the foot. He's in need of fast medical attention."

"Anything more?"

Jonah slipped out of his pale-blue lab coat, revealing a pin-striped suit that was out of style and fit him better five years ago.

"Conjecture on my part, but based on past history, I'd say the Lieutenant put two into body mass, and Trehearne popped one in the suspect's right foot."

"Sounds right to me," I said. "The manager told me MM's rental Ford Escape is missing, but that the parking valet still has the key-fob."

The younger of the CSIS operatives spoke for the first time since entering the room. "Not easy driving a car with a bullet through your foot. The fact that his car is gone indicates he's learned to drive with either foot."

The elder agent had a face you'd forget two seconds later: an unremarkable Mister Everybody, and Mister Nobody. On the other hand, his posture and stance gave away some military training or some past police experience. He spoke clearly and with an even tone, like a litigation lawyer questioning a witness on the stand.

"Lieutenant, you mentioned Mascara had taken a room in the hotel across the street, also on the sixth floor. In this room, behind the drape, there's a car camera suctioned to the right side of the window. He had surveillance on the street as well as on his second rented room. He was checking if his original cover was blown."

"I was wondering why the fetish for the sixth floor," I said.

"Mascara's actions show a lot of tradecraft knowledge. Rows of floors punched in the elevator is standard practice to confuse anyone tracking you."

"My RCMP contact told me he's a professional with at least eight hits to his credit."

"At the very least, you can double that number Lieutenant. We are involved, because he has worked with terrorist organizations, as well as international crime syndicates. He's an expert at what he does. You've been very lucky so far in tracking him, and in your confrontation with him."

"Good leg work, not luck, and I have my own reputation of always getting my man."

My boast didn't impress the Captain, who used one of his mock French swearwords, and added,

"*J'appréhende une tempête de merde.*"

"Don't worry about a shit storm, Captain. The RCMP promised to take care of the official paperwork crap for us."

"If you bring him in alive," Jean said. "With you, there are more bullets than handcuffs." He made a finger gun with his index, and thumb, and pointed at me.

I put my hands up to shoulder height, palms out. "It will depend on him."

The young CSIS agent said, "One thing *you* can depend on, Lieutenant Beaudry, is that he is no longer in town. So far, he's following standard operating procedures. If cornered in a room, don't wait for the enemy to get reinforcements, shoot your way out first. Attack is the best defense. Secondly, once there's been gunplay, get out of Dodge."

"He can't go far, we have a Bolo out on him."

"Exactly, *why*, you don't stay in the same city, Beaudry. Your local departments know about the warrant, but small town cops are not in the loop. They get the news later, if at all."

"You may be right. I'll go wider."

The tech people inventoried Mascara's luggage. A false bottom revealed a couple of syringes and vials that would go to the lab for analysis, a loaded spare pistol magazine, and a box of .380 ammo with twenty rounds missing.

"The good news is that our suspect has only five bullets left in his weapon," Jonah said.

"The other good news is that he's working alone, not in a team," the young CSIS agent said. "Else they would have booked adjoining rooms to have other escape routes."

"The additional good news is that he's wounded and will be on our radar as soon as he gets medical help," I said.

He added, "Don't count on that. As a pro, he has connections. He'd have set up for medical help before he confirmed the contract. The same to procure a silenced weapon, not an easy thing in Canada."

"I learn something new every day," I said.

The senior CSIS agent tugged his earlobe twice. His younger partner shut up and retreated from our circle. It was a signal I'd not yet learned from Roger and Nico's repertoire.

In the lining of his trench coat, we found a Spanish passport as well as a second French one—both under other aliases. In the event that he had driver's licenses under those names, I updated my *avis de recherche* and expanded the broadcast area.

Before we left, the senior Provincial officer gave me his card. Asking me next time to forget the *others* and call him direct.

"*Laisse faire les autres. La prochaine fois tu m'appelle.*"

Notwithstanding the pessimistic outlook from the Security Intelligence team, I had full confidence that the wounded Mascara Man's freedom was ending, and an easy capture was imminent.

In his escape, Mascara Man had abandoned his luggage, clothing, and sundries. It would leave him with meager resources. I was getting more confident.

Time would tell if my belief was a pipe dream or not.

- 24 -

An uncomfortable numbness in my right foot woke me. A heavy furry weight on my ankle had constricted the blood flow. I undraped Crackers from his warm spot. He showed his annoyance with an attempted nip at my hand.

I hobbled to the washroom, the pinpricks of returning circulation making me think of Mascara Man, and of his Trehearne-inflicted foot wound.

As I showered, my mind played back scenes from yesterday's confrontation with MM. Every time I arrested a suspect, with or without gunplay, I'd review my actions on what went well, or what went off track, to prepare answers for my boss O'Neil and for Infernal Affairs.

Pictures and sounds came from my memory frame by frame, as if I were watching a slide presentation. What a very odd thing to have my I.A. nemesis at my side this time.

Lorne had pulled the trigger seven times and managed to put only one bullet on target, into his opponent's foot. Something didn't jive. He had both hands on his weapon, albeit in a very poor stance, but with the amount of lead he let fly, it should have downed Mascara just by the odds of pure chance. An inexperienced person shooting fast will let the recoil pull up the weapon, and will wind up punching holes in the ceiling. How did Lorne manage that low shot and miss every other one?

Pat walked into the bathroom wearing only a pajama top and unashamedly plunked herself down to pee. I was going to have to get used to this living together thing.

"You look lost, you okay?" she said, as she finished her business.

"Reviewing yesterday. I told you that Lorne shot seven times from thirty feet away. He only managed one bullet in the guy's foot. I can't understand the odds of him missing so badly."

"Easy," Pat said, "he was shooting low because he had his eyes closed. At the academy, I was paired with Bridget, a recruit that did the same thing. She'd aim, then flinch her eyes shut. The gun would drop as she pulled the trigger.

It Took me a fortnight to break her from that habit."

"Ah crap, I think you may be right. I'm lucky I wasn't shot in the back."

"You're not so lucky this morning. There's not a crumb to be had for brekkie. But, I'm so glad you've no nasty holes in ya, we'll eat out. My treat."

* * *

Pat's fifteen-minute shower added to an hour and ten for hair, makeup, and choice of clothing, had me hungry enough to eat the cardboard menu.

"I'll have the Eggstravaganza with a side of baked beans," I said to Emilie, our server.

The fruit cup with the Greek yogurt was Pat's choice. She was still keeping a close watch on her weight.

"Still worried about the four ounces you gained on vacation?"

"You men can eat like ogres and not tip the scales. I'm telling ya, women will eat a cupcake and it'll settle straight on the hips."

"Never worry. I can suggest exercise for your hips."

"A snog and a jump is all yer after, you big muppet. What time are you going to the gym?"

"I'll give myself two hours to digest breakfast before I hit the weights."

"Good, I'll give us time to meet with Sandra."

I washed down a mouthful of toast and ham with a slurp of coffee. "Sandra?"

"Sandra, the designer, I told you about her last night. Were you not listening?"

"Ah, I vaguely remember you mentioning a decorator while you were undressing for bed."

"Interior designer. She's going to help us on the renovations."

"Us?"

"We're living together. I need your input. Overall layout, the placement of furniture, color schemes."

There was much more to this living together situation than I had first imagined.

* * *

Sandra was a petite five-foot ball of electric energy. Her multi-shades of blond and disheveled hairstyle reflected her bouncy personality. She showed up at Pat's house with several draft versions of floor plans, which she spread out enthusiastically on the dining room table.

"Patricia has given me her must-haves, and her like-to-haves. What does the Lieutenant consider essential?"

"I'm not on duty. Robert is okay." She gave me a hint of a smile and reached for a pencil.

"I like to cook, we need a decent kitchen, and I hate yellow, particularly on walls."

Sandra would have made a good interrogator. An hour later, she had a substantial list of my priorities for our joint living space, as well as my preferences on colors and furniture styles. She explained some of the technicalities of floor space, people movement, and workflow. Her planned layouts would assure comfortable daily living, while avoiding stepping on each other's toes. It surprised and reassured me.

I was now more enthusiastic about the new house. The plan would include a modern kitchen, separate bathrooms, his and hers walk-in closets, and a basement workshop for me. Later, I'd sneak in a hidden gun safe in my closet or workshop.

Pat said she would continue working with Sandra, "On a zillion details."

I told her I wanted to visit Trehearne in the hospital later in the day.

"He'll probably be discharged tomorrow. I don't want to visit him at home, we're not *that* friendly."

"We should be finished by two. Pick me up after your workout. I'd like to go with you," Pat said.

I headed to Antonio's gym. I needed exercise, and I needed to pry some critical information from my retired gunslinger friend.

Michael Kent

- 25 -

My wide frame, a genetic inheritance from husky French Canadian farmers, and a smidgen of stocky native Indian somewhere down the bloodline, plus my years of weight lifting, had given me bulk and muscles. My focus now centered on a cycle of improving strength. The regimen was increased weights, fewer reps, with emphasis not on individual body parts, but on overall power.

Antonio had acted as my strength coach for the assistance exercises. I was beating my personal bests that day.

During my workout, I had regaled him with the story of finding the Mascara Man, the shoot out, and Trehearne's bullet spraying technique.

"Your back-up was more dangerous than the hit-man." His comment, punctuated by a grunt and a scowl.

Under his watchful eye, I wiped down the equipment.

We sat on facing bench press boards.

"I don't want you to betray any trade secrets, but I'm curious about where he's going to get medical help," I said.

"The spy guy is right. Mascara's certainly not in Montreal. On the medical help, I won't tell you who, but I can give you the how."

"I'm still waiting on news from our biker friends. In the meantime, anything will help."

"It'll be a private clinic, a surgeon dentist, or a veterinarian."

"Veterinarian? Are you joking?"

"Don't underestimate. Nine times out of ten, a good vet can patch up a dog hit by a truck and have him wagging his tail the next day."

I remembered the information from Janet on Hui-Ju's new husband. It was worth a visit to someone in the profession.

Antonio faced me, but his eyes had drifted to his far right as he admired the spandexed tight rear of a woman on the treadmill across the aisle.

"You shot twice aiming for his chest, but it didn't stop him. You're a pretty fair shot, Beaudry.

I'd bet a twenty that he was wearing a protective vest. His worse problem is his foot, lots of small bone damage."

"*Pretty fair*, thanks for the compliment. There was blood spray on the wall next to him. I got one in for sure."

"He had his hands out. You probably nicked him in the armpit. That's the weak spot of soft armor. I remember acting as a bodyguard during an attempted army coup against my South-American client. The assassination squads were in full combat dress. The only vulnerable spots for pistol rounds were the face and armpit."

Antonio recounted his escape from that perilous situation. Surprisingly, this was the first time he'd spoken of his combat stories and shared some hard-learned survival tactics from his many years as a mercenary and hired gunslinger.

By the time I showered and changed, I was late for my phone call to Pat, but I lucked out.

"Sorry," she said. "We're out scouting furniture and appliances. I'm having a grand time. I totally forgot about the hospital visit. Call me when you're there, I'll wish him well myself."

* * *

I headed to the garish multi-colored cubes and rectangles that comprised the new Glen hospital complex. The city was in the process of rebuilding the downtown Ville-Marie expressway while at the same time demolishing the crumbling overhead turnpike around the new hospital site. It was a mess of trucks, cranes, orange cones, and detoured traffic. A car dealer showroom hung perilously at the edge of a man-made cliff above the construction site.
It was probably no longer a prime location for that business.

By pure chance, and some assertive driving, I managed to find the entrance to the hospital underground parking. More good luck in the form of a friendly volunteer greeter, who gave me directions to Lorne's room.

Trehearne sat upright, reading a document, a small pile of files stacked at the foot of his bed.

"Can't live without the paperwork, can you?"

"I'd not recognize you without the sarcasm, Lieutenant."

"We're now warfare buddies. You can call me Robert. But not in public."

"The doctor is releasing me tomorrow, but the office put me on leave for a month because I'm booked for physio. My wife is in a dither—she says I'll be a bad patient and underfoot at home."

I speed-dialed Pat's number.

When she answered, I said, "Here he is."

Then I handed the phone to Lorne. She hung up after speaking to him.

"Exceptionally thoughtful of your girlfriend to wish me well. I'm touched. She said she was in an appliance store and would call you later."

Lorne returned my Android.

"She thanked me for protecting you. I don't understand."

Trehearne shook the paper in his hand.

"The scene report says I shot seven times and hit our suspect in the foot. I can't believe seven times. I do believe that I'm a poor shot. I muffed target qualification last month."

"Pat thanked you because you did protect me. In the stress of the situation, you sprayed bullets at the Mascara Man. At that moment you seemed the most dangerous opponent and he turned his attention on you, not on me."

Lorne looked at the report again. "Seven shots?"

"Yes, and I do thank you. I owe you one. When you're feeling better, we'll go to the range. In no time I'll have you punching holes in the black."

"I...I don't know what to say. This is so unexpected."

I shook his hand and left before he got teary-eyed.

My good luck stayed with me for lunchtime. On the main floor, I found a food court and restaurants as if I was in a shopping center, not a hospital.

I chose from the Subway menu.

I texted Pat writing that I'd meet her for supper. The Glen is close the Champlain Bridge My next logical stop, would be Hui-Ju's home. I hoped her husband would know of rumored double duty vets.

- 26 -

The construction mess around the bridge included new exits, closed exits, and detours. Slightly disoriented, I took the wrong road. Pat would have said I was lost, and I would have commented, "I never get lost, only confused." The only comment today was my GPS's incessant *recalculating* announcement.

I navigated to Route 30 eastbound toward Boucherville and Sorel. I was on track, and my GPS robot female voice seemed content. With a few twists and turns, she led me to the posh Boucherville development of *Le Boisé,* comprised entirely of multi-million-dollar residences.

I couldn't miss the home. A flame-red moving van filled the driveway of Hui-Ju and Kendall Jardine's mid-sized castle. As if they were a line of ants, men clad in blue overalls were busy transporting furniture from the house to the eighteen-wheeler.

Avoiding the march of out-coming movers, I walked sideways through the double front door into the foyer.

One of the blue men had stopped to adjust his forearm lifting straps. I did my badge flip.

"Where's the lady?"

"Kitchen, turn right from the living room."

I found Hui-Ju seated in a breakfast nook off the main kitchen. She was on the phone, speaking in rapid Mandarin, her left forearm and hand immobilized in a cast, a pink sling hanging loose around her neck. With a smile and a nod, she motioned for me to sit across from her. She spoke a few more sentences, and then ended her phone conversation.

I pointed at her cast. "What happened?"

"We were in a local restaurant. Jimmy spilled his juice onto one of our guest's lap. Kendall was furious. I stood up to restrain him from striking Jimmy. My dear husband, true to himself, pushed me aside. I fell against a table." She raised her left arm, "Compound fracture."

"Ouch. You pressing charges this time?"

"Divorce papers already filed and delivered. Everyone was appalled that he'd try to strike a child, and be so brutal with me. I have affidavits from four witnesses at our table, and two from bystanders."

"You moving out, or is he?"

"Both. Nearly all of the furniture is mine from my last marriage. The house is fifty percent mine and will be for sale as of next Monday."

"Big changes. You okay?"

"I'll be fine. I'm surprised to see you here. You found out from the local police?"

"I planned to check up on you, but, in all honesty, I'm here because I need to ask your husband some questions pertaining to his business."

"He's moping on the rear deck. I hope you find the *dànténg* guilty of many crimes and you can put him away for a long time."

I know nothing of Mandarin, but I was certain the word she used was not a compliment.

"Hui-Ju, apart from ill manners and stupidity, so far as I know, his only guilt is of not appreciating a beautiful, intelligent woman."

My sloppy compliment didn't score any brownie points. She raised her gaze to the ceiling and pointed to the patio door.

I found him at the edge of the pool installed in an oversized upholstered rocking patio chair.

Kendall Jardine was a balding, egg-shaped man, wearing what I recognized as a two-thousand-dollar Armani suit. Time spent with my clotheshorse friend Nico was rubbing off on me.

Although the sun was barely over the yardarm, he sipped from a large tumbler of amber liquid.

A half-empty bottle of Famous Grouse sat at his feet.

I performed my artful badge flip.

"Mister Jardine, I'm Lieutenant Robert Beaudry, and I need to talk to you."

"I've said everything I have to say. Speak to my lawyer."

I pulled up a straight-backed version of his chair and sat facing him.

"This has nothing to do with your personal life."

"I no longer have a personal life." He took a sip of his drink. "I'm screwed. I don't even have a bed to sleep in."

"I don't know what happened in your personal life," I lied. "I need some information pertaining to a case I'm working on."

Jardine lowered his head, the sun glinting off his bald spot. "Is this more shit? I don't think I can stand more shit."

"On the contrary, if you can help me, you may earn very favorable comments from a homicide detective." I shrugged. "Never know when that can come in handy."

"A homicide—this *is* more deep shit isn't it?"

He jerked his arm as if he either wanted to toss his drink at me, or gulp it down in one swallow. I grabbed his wrist, preventing him from doing either.

I felt him tremble. He made a coughing sound and tears flowed from his eyes.

He tilted forward and seemed to shrink inside his fancy suit. I stood and put my hands on his shoulders to steady him. "Take it easy, whoa horsey."

* * *

Jardine had started the new bottle of scotch when the movers had arrived early in the morning. He was one of those disconsolate drunks that oozed sadness instead of sweat. He seemed to have a twisted version of his marriage to Hui-Ju, one where *he* was the victim. It took twenty minutes of patient listening, and two cups of coffee before I was able to ask him about his clinic and if he knew of any vets who patched up criminals as a sideline.

"I worked hard for the last twenty-three years building a successful business. I know what I'm doing. All of my staff are irreproachable."

"You misunderstood my question. I'm not after anyone in your clinics."

"I should hope not. I can vouch for all of them. Anton had a bit of a drinking problem, but he's in AA and—"

I put my open palm in front of his face.

"Let's restart this conversation. In all of your many years in business, have you had knowledge, or have you heard rumors of any vets that have patched up bullet or knife wounds, or have helped criminals with drugs—or have done anything else shady?"

"I did five years of university training to obtain my DVM. It's an honorable profession. We have tons of government regulations to comply with—"

I put my hand up again. "That's why I'm here *Doctor* Jardine. I need help from an expert. Do you have doubts about any off-Montreal Island vets?"

"Well, of course I know many people in the field. All good people." He bent to look at the bottle of booze I had slid under my chair. "Exception made for Bad Boy Brown."

"Bad Boy Brown?"

"His real name is Antoine Lebrun. Calls himself Tony Brown, thinks he's a friggin' rock star.

"What makes you think he's doing something illegal?"

"I know how many clients you need and pet supplies you have to sell to make a good living. I've built two successful clinics."

"So?"

"So, he has a shitty little shop on the banks of the Richelieu River and does house calls in a souped up Range Rover."

I was about to give up. I stood up and stretched my legs. "So he likes fancy cars."

"Fancy isn't the word. He built a ten-room house across from the river, has a forty-foot sailboat. ATVs, snowmobiles, his wife drives a new Volvo four-by-four. Rumors are he launders dirty money."

Tolstoy wrote that the two most powerful warriors were patience and time. I had neither. I swallowed my annoyance with Jardine and managed to get the address for Brown's clinic.

He wrote it on the back of his business card and told me he'd give me a discount on pet food.

On my way out, Hui-Ju asked if I had caught my suspect.

"We're searching for the red motorcycle. Thanks for Jimmy's help."

"Oh, oh, I forgot to tell you, Jimmy hates the color orange. He could have colored the bike red, instead of orange."

I should have given Manny Agnant an update, adding what Vanessa told me in our conversation at the airport.

Michael Kent

- 27 -

I dutifully followed the vocal instructions of my GPS lady as she led me to exit 112 of the TransCanada, then to a secondary road snaking along the Richelieu River. Ten kilometers southbound, I found Brown's veterinary center across from a shopping mall at the intersection of Route 116 and Richelieu Street.

Contrary to Jardine's description of, "A crappy little clinic." The low modern building looked new and attractive. The window sign indicated *Fermé - Closed*. A silver Range Rover sat next to the entrance, front facing, and badly overlapping the parking lines. The driver mustn't be OCD, I thought to myself as my phone rang.

Antonio's gruff voice assailed me from the car speakers. "Where are you?"

I lowered the volume. "In front of *Paradis des Animaux,* A vet clinic along the Richelieu River."

"I've made some inquires. That place is on my list. Do you have back-up?"

"Didn't think I needed to. Animals love me."

"Our friends delivered a phone. Wait for me. I'll bring it to you."

I stepped out of my Jeep and walked to the front of the Range Rover. The hood was cool to the touch. Maybe the door sign was telling the truth. I went back to my car and parked sideways, blocking the Range Rover.

Waiting patiently isn't one of my strong points. I decided I could chance a walk across the street to the bakery.

Antonio arrived forty-six minutes and four doughnuts later. I slipped into his Mercedes with my open box.

"I still have two left."

In exchange for an iPhone, he took the maple walnut.

"They cloned the guy's phone," he said.

"This is a clone of Lamarsh's phone?"

"I just said that. Stop dropping crumbs on my upholstery and listen. They added a viral surprise."

"Umm."

"You'll have to send a text to Mascara's phone. When he reads it, the spyware will install itself."

I licked jelly from my fingers. "What does the program do?"

"It'll map out what cell tower his phone is pinging off of. The closer we get, the more precise it'll be."

"Let's check out the vet first," I said. "It may narrow our search."

The clinic's front door was unlocked. I took point as Antonio pulled out a .50 cal. Desert Eagle from under his jacket.

"Are you afraid of a rabid elephant?"

"Just grabbed the first thing in the safe."

I stepped into the reception area. "This is the police, anybody here?"

I heard a thump from the rear of the building.

We walked slow and silent down the corridor, checking each room, one office, and three examination cubicles.

"Your Mascara Man may be recuperating here," Antonio whispered, pointing to a door marked *Surgery*.

I took the hinge side. Antonio turned the knob and pushed the door open with his oversized pistol.

"We're coming in armed. Stay where you are and put your hands on your head. You move, you die," I said.

My warning was superfluous. The man and woman in the room were unable to put their hands on their heads. Both wore pale blue scrubs and lay on the floor back to back, gagged and as bound up tight as two fish caught in a trawler net.

I flipped open my penknife, then cut the tape and gauze from the man's gag.

"Tony Brown, I presume."

"Untie me and my wife, untie, untie." He added a French swearword that my boss had yet to use.

"You have to earn your freedom first."

I scrolled the pictures in my phone to the last known disguised Mascara Man mock up.

"The mustache may be different. This the guy that tied you up?"

"A couple of masked men came in to steal drugs, dunno what they looked like. Untie us."

"If that's the story you're going with, I think it's a bad choice."

"He'll come back and kill us both."

"Ooops, the story's changing already."

"We know nothing. Untie us, please. My legs hurt. Is Joanie okay?"

"If you're referring to the lady tied to your back, she's a bit red in the face but she's breathing."

"You're cops. You have to untie us."

"Did I say we were cops? I'm no longer sure. I must have the same memory problem that plagues you."

"I can't tell you anything."

"He must have left not long ago. Neither of you have pissed yourselves yet."

"Fuck, fuck."

"I don't think that's in the cards either. Not the way you're trussed up."

"You don't understand."

"Oh, *yes* I do. I'm the one that put a bullet in his armpit. He also has one through his right foot. He told you, if you talk, he'll come back to kill you and your family. That won't happen, because I'll get him first."

Brown sighed. "No armpit, bullet grazed his right triceps."

"And my second shot hit his Kevlar vest."

He nodded, "Big ugly bruise an inch above his nipple."

We made a deal with Brown, aka Lebrun. He gave us the details of his medical work on the Mascara Man, told us we missed him by an hour and twenty minutes and that he was heading to a local airport. He was unsure if it was the large civil Saint Hubert airport or a small club runway such as Saint Mathias or Beloeil. Our part of the bargain was to re-gag him, use his office phone to call the local station and report masked men entering the clinic. Tony would stick to his drug burglary story and avoid an inquiry into his secondary business.

The solution was far removed from my police rulebook, but Antonio and Brown agreed on the plan. It wouldn't dry up medical help for some of Antonio's friends still in the mercenary business.

We wiped down everything we had touched as if we were never there.

- 28 -

From the mall parking lot across the street from the clinic, I sent a text to the Mascara Man's phone.

"Heard of hotel prob. U ok to finish?"

On the clone, I saw his answer as he typed.

'My brother will finish n/c.'

I showed Antonio the reply. "He's sending another hitter to finish the contract. He's paying the fee."

"Very professional of him," Antonio said. "Give it a minute or so, and then call him. It's on speed dial nine. The spyware will activate and we'll get a map position."

Across the street, two Beloeil patrol cars rolled up to Brown's clinic—Code Two, no sirens, or lights.

"Eleven minutes. I'll bet it's faster than a Montreal response," Antonio said.

"The station is probably two blocks away." I put my finger across my lips. "I'm calling him."

My call would register on Mascara's phone as from Lamarsh, the Rock Machine's enforcer.

He answered on the third ring. The software kicked in and a map appeared on my screen. I made the background noise of a bad connection by crumpling a doughnut wrapper over the microphone, then hung up.

I moved the map view with my index finger.

"It shows a blue circle around a star. North of here. Next to the T-Can."

Antonio snatched the phone from my hand and resized the map.

"Beloeil airport, we use my car. I have vests in the trunk."

Ensconced in the passenger seat of Antonio's AMG S-class, I held the clone phone in one hand. In the other, I dialed Pat's number from mine.

As soon as she answered, I spoke. "I've got a hot lead on the Hit-Man. Don't think I'll make it for supper, sorry."

"Not a bother. I've had a full day. I'm failed. Don't dare get yourself hurt, I'd not forgive ya."

"Antonio is my back-up."

"That's a comfort."

I promised to wake her with a kiss when I got home. She told me not to bother. Antonio sped us up a country road shortcut, shaking his head at my kissy-kiss goodbye.

* * *

Beloeil airport was a short paved private strip, surrounded by farmland. At the southeast, the runway all but abutted the T-Can highway and the northwest end was in the shadow of Mount Saint-Hilaire.

For a small airport, there were a surprising number of hangars along the runway. The first and largest building housed a flight school. We parked in front of the office steps.

"Learning here must be a challenge to students." Antonio pointed to the windsock at forty-five degrees to the airstrip. "Let me tell you that a crosswind landing with a thousand-foot mountain at the other end of your runway makes a missed approach interesting."

"I didn't know you were a pilot."

"Many years ago, in the African bush."

As soon as we entered the building, a young man dressed in rumpled mechanic's coveralls rushed up to us from his post behind the service counter. He had an acne scarred face and a worried look.

"You the pilot?"

"No, I'm the detective." I did my badge flip.

"No, no. He said he'd kill Paul and Jacques if we called the cops. No, no, no. This is not good."

From my phone, I showed him the Mascara Man picture. "This the man?"

"No, he's a hunched crazy old man with a mop of white hair. He's wild eyed. He limped into the hanger and started waving a big gun, said he wanted a pilot immediately."

"He has a limp?"

"Yes, he has some kind of plastic brace on his right foot."

"We got him," I said to Antonio.

"He's a nut case. I told him our instructors are in the practice zone flying with students. He shoved the gun in my mouth. I nearly shit myself. He told me to get a pilot or he'd kill all of us."

"When was that?"

"Less than twenty minutes ago. I called our other school at Sorel to get another pilot. He should be here by now."

"Where's the gunman?"

"In the second hangar next door. The big one. They're prepping the PA forty-four for flight."

"Twin engine Piper?" Antonio asked.

"Yeah, the green and white Seminole. We just finished the annual. We were doing the final inspection."

"I don't like the hostage situation, Robert. I think you'd better get official help. This could go south real fast."

Our mechanic looked as if he was about to up-chuck his lunch.

"You better sit down," I said. "Is there a phone in the hangar?"

"Yeah." He pointed to the desk phone on the counter. "Just dial two. It's a direct extension."

I pulled out the business card the Provincial Police had given me in Mascara's room and called the number using my cell.

"Captain Hébert, this is Lieutenant Beaudry. I have the Mascara Man holding hostages at Beloeil Airport. You interested?"

"Are the horses there?"

"Horses?"

"RCMP."

"No, you asked me to call you first. I need back-up fast."

"You're in luck. We have a helicopter and a SWAT team on a terrorist simulation exercise at the old military college in Saint-Jean, minutes from you."

Hébert hung up as abruptly as my boss does. Maybe it was part of the training for the Captain stripes.

"SWAT is on the way. We have to stall. You're the designated pilot," I said to Antonio.

"What's your name?" I asked the mechanic.

"Bert."

"Okay, Bert, let's save your friends. Call the hangar. Tell him the pilot is here and he needs to talk to him."

Bert dialed the extension.

Pilot's here, wants to talk to you." His hand shook when he gave the handset to Antonio. Not risking the speakerphone, we heard only one side of the conversation.

"They told me this was a medical emergency flight. What's the problem, and where are we going?"

"Business emergency to Burlington? Oh, that's less of a panic. I have to check the weather. There's a cold front coming in, and I have to file an ADCUS flight plan."

"No, it's not far. A twenty-minute flight, but we can't cross the U.S. border without a flight plan. They'll scramble jets to force us down."

"You said you have your passport, so no problem as long as you're not bringing anything illegal."

"How are you paying for this?"

"Cash is fine, if you don't need a receipt, we won't charge tax."

Antonio walked to the framed chart on the wall behind the counter. "The plane is two hundred and ninety-nine per hour, wet and insured. I need two fifty for the flight."

"Rounded out, we're looking at six hundred."

"Well, because it includes time on the ground at Burlington."

Antonio looked at me and shrugged his shoulders.

"Yeah, you can have them fuel up while I finish the paperwork." Antonio hung up the extension.

"He knows he's running out of time," I said. "I'm not sure if we can stall long enough for SWAT to get into position."

Antonio shook his head. "Even surrounded by a SWAT team, he may go out shooting."

"I think he has only five rounds left in his weapon."

"It's enough to kill five people, Robert. He's seen *you*. I have to take point on this."

The front of the flight school counter was a glass showcase with tee-shirts, flight jackets, aircraft logo badges, patches, and a stack of flight instruction manuals.

Antonio pointed to worried faced Bert, then to the counter.

"Find me a flight jacket in size large." He tossed me his key fob. "Get the vests from my car. Under the trunk mat."

Antonio had had a body shop remodel the spare tire compartment of his AMG to fit vests, a take-apart Sig SG550 sniper rifle, and a box of ammo.

As I closed the trunk lid, the large door of the next hangar folded out and upward.

I ran back to the office, hopeful that no one in the next building saw me.

A small red tractor pulled out a shiny new-looking, low-wing, twin-engine T-tail plane from the hangar, and maneuvered it to the gas pumps between the office and the second building.

Antonio wore his Kevlar vest under a *Pilots do it higher* logo tee-shirt, and an unzipped tan flight jacket. He carried a rectangular briefcase and a clipboard with some type of phone-sized computer attached to it. He looked perfect for the part.

"He's an expert at disguises and subterfuge. You have to play your role to perfection, Antonio."

I moved a chair to the runway-facing window and assembled the scoped rifle.

"Set the selector to three," Antonio said. "If the window doesn't open, you'll have to blast through it. Your first round will be deflected off target. Don't shoot unless I'm down or he has a draw on me."

One of the mechanics fueled the plane. I lined up the scope on the cabin. A man dressed in overalls sat next to a man with bushy white hair.

"It's him. He can change hairdos and add make-up all he wants, but he can't change his eyes," I said. "I've seen that look from up close."

Antonio crouched beside me. I handed him the rifle.

"The second mechanic is in the pilot seat to help steer the plane," he said. "A Seminole's cabin door is on the passenger side. Mascara has to exit the plane to let me sit in the pilot seat."

"He steps out, I can nail him," I said.

"You weren't listening. I said not to shoot unless I'm down. I have a plan that may take him alive."

Antonio asked Bert to find adhesive tape. He came back with two rolls of glass cloth aerospace tape.

Using a couple of easers as spacers, Antonio taped his pistol to the back edge of his clipboard. He held his contraption with three fingers around the pistol, his index in the trigger guard and his thumb over the clipboard. When he positioned it down next to his leg, computer side front, it looked perfectly normal, the weapon entirely hidden.

"I think you've done this before," I said.

"Something similar, on the principle that you can't outdraw a drawn gun. The downside is that I get only one shot. The taped slide won't let the gun eject properly. If this doesn't work, put the crosshairs on his nose."

"I'll be ready."

Antonio walked out only when the first mechanic dragged the gas hose around to the left side tank, away from the line of fire and the planned surprise move against Mascara.

Antonio strutted up to the plane, dropped his flight case under the wing, and told Mascara to exit for a minute to permit the pilot-for-mechanic seat change. Mascara held onto the top of the open door as he gingerly put his right foot on the walk strip of the wing root. Antonio, still holding onto his gimmicked clipboard, politely offered his left hand to Mascara. As their hands clasped, Antonio yanked Mascara off the wing, flipping him onto his back on the tarmac. It *wasn't* the hit-man's lucky day. As he plunged off the wing, his weapon flew from his jacket and landed five or six feet to his right. Antonio knelt beside his captive, the hidden pistol now pointing down. Mascara's left hand was pinned under Antonio's knee, his right hand still restrained by a strong grip.

I dropped the rifle, drew my sidearm, and rushed to the scene, arriving next to Mascara Man and Antonio to the beat of helicopter blades coming from the mountain end of the runway.

- 29 -

With a relieved smile on my face, I cuffed our international hit man.

"There're going to extradite your disguised ass to Germany, old man."

"My name is Aref, and it's a long trip to a German prison," he said. "Many things can happen."

Antonio hid his weaponized clipboard in the flight case, and then bent close to Aref, who lay face forward on the wing, his feet dangling over the ailerons.

"If you escape, don't come back to Quebec. I'll kill you," he whispered.

The outsized multi-windowed helicopter landed with a graceful pivot, crossways onto the runway numbers. The tactical team jumped out of the Provincial Police aircraft, their weapons pointing at us.

I held one hand on my head, the other straight up, holding my shield.

I yelled, "Stand down, stand down, he's captured."

They used a stretcher from the helicopter to strap down and move Aref, the Mascara Man. His right foot had bled through his bandages and he had suffered a broken elbow from his tussle with Antonio.

While they sorted things out, I stood next to Bert and Antonio. Out of earshot from the officers, I coached them on my scenario.

Waiting for the brass to arrive, four of the ten-man SWAT team kept everyone captive in the flight school office. Two had accompanied Aref in the ambulance to a local hospital; the others stood guard around the buildings.

They had confiscated my weapon, the SIG rifle, and insisted we stay put. Exception made for Antonio, who had managed to ingratiate himself with the police pilot. They were both chatting away in the big Agusta helicopter.

After an irritating forty-five-minute wait, Captain Hébert arrived with another captain, and a lieutenant, neither of whom was introduced.

They appeared pleased that I hadn't informed the RCMP nor CSIS, but insisted on a detailed review of the events leading to the capture. The unnamed lieutenant held his phone out to record my conversation.

I perched on the service counter. Bert stood behind it.

"A few minutes past four this afternoon, Aref, the Mascara Man, burst into the hangar to our left, as three mechanics were doing the final checks on a twin Piper Seneca after its annual inspection and maintenance."

Captain Hébert made a fast clockwise motion with his index finger. I ignored it, and continued at the same pace.

"Aref insisted on finding a pilot for a flight to the U.S. Bert, Paul, and Jacques were held at gunpoint and threatened with death if they could not meet his request."

Hébert glared at me. "Bert was turned loose to call a freelance instructor. He called Karl, a pilot and an undercover narcotics cop he knew."

"Where's Karl?" asked Hébert.

"Talking business with your helicopter jockey. To shorten the story, Karl, who's a friend of mine and a narcotics officer in deep cover—unable to reveal his true identity, to the local police, or even to you guys—called me. He knew I was in Boucherville interviewing a witness in another case. We met, drove here, stalled the Mascara Man until your team arrived and captured him."

The SWAT leader looked at me with question marks dripping from his eyes.

"Since of course, I have no jurisdiction here."

Captain Hébert glowed as he congratulated both me, and his dumbfounded SWAT team leader.

Delighted to upstage both the RCMP and CSIS, he said that he expected all the paperwork to conform to my story.

The saying that luck walks and bullshit flies, was very true today. B.S. magically turns into truth when it fits the politics of the moment. Even if weapons of mass destruction aren't found.

It was eight-twenty in the evening when everyone departed: SWAT back to the military base for a debriefing, Hébert and his cronies to I didn't know where, Bert, and his mechanic friends to the local *brasserie* for beers and pumped up versions of their day's adventure with their drinking buddies.

As we slid into Antonio's car, he said,
"I presume you're starving."
"I can hardly stand up."

"On our drive over, I saw a good looking French restaurant along the river road. It's my gas so you pay for supper."

"I'm too weak to argue. Besides, the pilot is always in command."

Michael Kent

- 30 -

I stepped into Pat's bedroom just before one a.m. She sat up in bed as I undressed.

"I was beginning to worry. I see no holes, nor fresh scars. It's a relief, it is."

"Not a scratch. I have to tell you about my very lucky day."

One leg over mine, she rested her head on my shoulder as I recounted my day. Somewhere in my telling, a delicate snore hinted that I'd continue the second chapter tomorrow morning.

Sunday is supposed to be a day of rest. I had planned to lounge in bed, cuddling with Pat; however, cats don't observe human calendars or timetables.

The bedside clock read five forty-two a.m. when Crackers decided it was breakfast time.

First, he tried to open my right eyelid with his paw.

"I wanna sleep," I mumbled, and turned over.

He then licked the top and back of my head. The grooming progressed to some hair pulling. I moved him to the foot of the bed and folded the edge of the comforter over him. Undaunted, he came back and bit the top of my ear.

Pat turned to my siade."What time'z ziz it?"

"Too early to get up, I have to feed the furry monster."

I pulled down her pajama top and gave Pat a titty kiss.

"Mark my spot, I'll be back."

I came back to the bedroom as Pat walked out of the bathroom. Naked, she slid back into bed and held a corner of the comforter up for me.

"Last night, yourself was telling me about his lucky day. You must be charmed. I woke randy this morning."

Overdressed for the occasion, I dropped the boxers and scrambled in beside her.

* * *

We had a very late breakfast. While I prepared scrambled eggs, roasted some peppers, tomato slices, and fried some bacon, Pat told me about her shopping excursion with Sandra, our decorating expert.

"I have pictures of the furniture and of the accessory stuff that I loved best. After breakfast, we'll make a purchase list. I may have to take you up on your investment offer."

I washed, then sliced some fresh fruits, and added the bowl to the setting on the kitchen table.

Pat made herself a plate with some of the fruit, added a yogurt, and binged on half of a multi-wheat toast.

"You fell asleep before I finished my story of yesterday."

"I heard you and Antonio captured the Mascara killer. Fair game to both of you. What I've not heard recently is what you're doing for your friend Nico."

"I have a lead. I called Manny twice while you were in the shower. It goes direct to voicemail and he hasn't called me back."

"A lead?"

"The lab said the rifle we found in the dumpster is the murder weapon. We have a description of the kid that tossed it, but we had the wrong color for his motorcycle."

Pat stole the other half of a toast from my plate.

"The red motorbike you were looking for?"

"The new red is orange."

She took a delicate bite of the toast. "You're talking riddles."

I related part of the conversation I had with Hui-Ju, adding the snippet of information from my airport conversation with Vanessa.

Pat stopped eating and shook her index finger at me. "I'm after telling you, don't wait for Manny. You know he may return his calls only Monday, *if* he does."

* * *

I took Pat's advice and headed to Nico's house. On the way, I grabbed a box of cannolis and some other heavily caloried goodies from an Italian pastry shop.

When she opened her front door, I handed the box to Carmen.

"Sunday treat for the girls."

"This is a surprise. *Prego, prego*. We're in the kitchen. Where's Patricia?"

"I'm afraid this isn't only a social call. I have to speak with Adrianna."

"Oh no. She's in the guest bedroom, *sperare che,* she's still sleeping. We've had a hard time since Annick talked to her. *Povera bambina* is having a breakdown."

"*Annick,* came to see Adrianna?"

Carmen stopped in mid-stride and turned to me, her hand to her mouth.

"Is something wrong?"

"I don't know yet. When was Annick here?"

"Yesterday morning. Just before she left for the airport."

I pointed to the rarely used living room.

"We better sit down and talk."

Apparently Annick had told Carmen she was going on a trip to Italy to help a cousin, owner of a fair sized hotel in Ventimiglia—a small border town close the French Riviera. She wanted to offer Adrianna a break from the problems at home, joining her for a month-long vacation in Italy with excursions to Provence.

"Two minutes after Annick was in the guest room, Adrianna was crying," Carmen said. "Worse than crying, howling."

"That doesn't sound like a reaction to a trip to the Riviera," I said.

"I rushed to the room, but they had locked the door. Annick came out when I threatened to knock the door down."

"What did Annick say?"

"Nothing, she rushed out without saying even goodbye. Adrianna was in a fit, rolling on the floor and hitting herself in the face."

"Ouch, this is a delicate situation. I don't want to make things worse for Adrianna. I'm going ask Roger to come over."

"You think she needs a psychologist?"

"I think he's the only person that should talk to her at the moment. It sounds as if she's more fragile than your fine china."

- 31 -

Roger's intervention with Adrianna lasted three long hours. I had asked Carmen if I could do something for her, rearrange furniture, add shelves to a cabinet, anything. She kept me busy by feeding me, and then had me drive the girls to soccer practice.

Ten minutes after my return, Roger stepped out of the guest bedroom.

"I gave her a mild sedative. Let her sleep," he said to Carmen. He rummaged in his wallet and handed her a business card.

"Leonard Zicherman is a highly recommended friend of mine from the Jewish General. She needs a lot of professional help."

"Is she sick?"

"She's going through an emotional crisis that may scar her for life."

Roger looked at me and covertly tugged his earlobe.

"Carmen, Robert and I have a meeting at the office. I'll ask Leonard to phone you today."

When we left, Carmen had a very worried look on her face. Roger promised he'd call later to follow up on Adrianna's condition.

Roger sat in the passenger seat of my Jeep. I had tried to ask him what Adrianna's problem was, but he waved me off.

"First things first," he said, dialing his phone.

"Aliza, it's Roger Lamont, sorry to disturb you. Is Leonard around?"

Roger put his hand over the microphone.

"Robert, I'll give the nine-one-one after my call, relax."

"Leonard—no this is business. I have an emergency request. Adrianna, fifteen years old. Close family to my partner Nico. High trauma, with potential self-mutilation. The causal event is that she's indirectly responsible for the recent murder of her father."

"Ah, rats," I said.

Roger gave me his *professor* stare and I shut up while he finished his conversation with his psychiatrist friend.

When he hung up, he turned to me.

"Unknown to her strict parents, Adrianna dated the motorcycle boy you're looking for," Roger said.

"I had that part pretty well figured out."

Roger gave me the *look* again. I let him finish without interruption.

"She didn't confirm, but I'd guess there was some sexual experimentation. The boy, Peter Reid, was too aggressive and forceful. It scared her, and she broke it off. Peter, in her words, went weirdo. She made herself blameless by saying her father found out about her dating and forbade it."

"Holy saints in heaven."

"I think Pat is rubbing off on you," Roger said.

"You got an address on the Reid kid?"

Roger handed me a folded paper.

"Adrianna wrote it down on the day of the murder. She couldn't bring herself to give it to Nico. She's in a total conflict with herself."

* * *

The Reid house was in the East end of Montreal in the Anjou borough, a residential neighborhood of recently built, midsized semi-detached town houses.

During my drive, Manny returned my calls. He was in the emergency ward waiting on the results of his X-ray. He predicted a broken leg from a bad skateboard move. I brought him up to date and told him that I'd take care of interviewing the suspect.

When I rang, a man and a woman answered the door. They stood next to each other as if glued at the hips.

He had a sourpuss face and little pig eyes. She had no makeup on her sad face, her eyes cast downward like a scolded child.

My badge flip elicited an immediate response.

"Finally, someone listened," said the man.

"You the parents of Peter Reid?"

"Yes, of course. We've been shuttled around on the phone to most of your departments. I'm *surprised* they finally took us seriously."

"I'm sorry Mr. Reid, but you'll have to give me the story again."

"My name's Charles. I must had said that six times today. Don't you cops talk to each other?"

"I just got the call. I'm on my day off. I didn't pass by the office," I lied.

We sat at the kitchen table. The coffee she served me was good. It helped clear my overstuffed feeling from Carmen's treats.

"Pete placed an online add to sell his bike. About time he got rid of that noisy thing," Charles, the father said. "Two big guys showed up Saturday morning. Pete said they were going to try the bike out on a dirt trail. They placed the bike in the back of their SUV, and he left with them."

He looked at me, his lips curled back as if to dare me to challenge what he was about to say. His wife was still staring downward.

"Pete's high strung, and he's been in a bit of trouble before. He comes in late sometimes, but he always comes home—always."

I had chills running up and down my back. I felt as if Annick was rubbing an ice cube along my spine. I recalled her arrogant tone when she said,

"Get off your high horse, Robert. We just want justice to be done."

"You called to report him missing?"

"Hell yes, isn't that why you're here?"

I gave him my card.

"I'm not from missing persons. I'm a homicide detective."

His wife suddenly ended her analysis of the floor tiles. She looked at her husband, her eyes watery.

"You ridiculed me when I said that there were danger vibes around the men that came for the bike. I saw a gravestone in the tea leaves this morning." She turned to me. "My son is dead, isn't he?"

"I don't know, ma'am, I just came to ask him some questions. He may be a witness in a murder."

Charles stood up and leaned over me, his clenched fists hitting the tabletop.

"Are you telling me you're not going to help find him?"

I grabbed and held his wrists. "Sit down. Let's work this out together."

He tried pulling his hands out of my grip but found them firmly glued to the tabletop. His face flamed red and veins bulged around his temples. After a few tries he flopped back into his chair like a deflated balloon.

"On the contrary, Charles, I take it very personally when one of my important witnesses suddenly disappears."

"Pete's an asshole, but he's my only son."

"Did you get the license number of the SUV?"

"It was across the street. I didn't have my glasses on. It started with an F, a black Escalade."

I didn't get much more. Both of them withdrew into a progressive sadness, as if they were reading my suspicions. Their description of the men, were "scary big guys." That would include many of my friends, as well as most of the wanted pictures posted at every precinct.

When I left the Reid's I was frustrated and angry. I imagined devil-girl Annick, sipping a glass of wine somewhere pleasant, with a satisfied smirk on her face.

- *32* -

My boss had reluctantly agreed to the Monday afternoon meeting. Nico, visibly jet lagged, Roger, who had driven him from the airport, their boss the vociferous Captain Falco, James Farrow from missing persons, Manny Agnant, a colorfully decorated plaster cast on his left leg, his crutches on the chair beside him, and I, sat around a boardroom table at headquarters.

I summarized the Aldo murder case, editing out some of my involvement and highlighting Manny's, but stressing my bar meeting with Annick. I detailed my Sunday visit to Nico's house to see how Carmen and the girls were doing, then my call to Roger, and his help with the distraught Adrianna.

When I spoke of our *accidental* discovery of Peter Reid and our suspicions that he murdered Aldo because of what Adrianna had said, Nico rested his forehead on the table, his tears dripping on the glass top.

"I've opened a personal case file on Peter Reid," I said. "It's too much of a suspicious disappearance. I think he's paid for Aldo's murder."

My boss, Captain O'Neil, interjected.

"There's no such thing as a personal case file. You have no facts, only suspicions. We have no body, so no murder, so no case. I put a stack of cold cases on your desk. If you want to waste your time on this, then your terminology is correct—it'll be on your personal time."

"I have the case. I leave it unsolved for now," Manny said.

"For me, it's another missing person on my list," Sergeant Farrow said.

Aldo stood up, a sad look in his eyes. "Robert, we go back a long time my friend, but I can't deny my Italian heritage, we'll have different views on this. *In fin die conti,* I'm satisfied with this ending."

Captain Falco said, "Maybe it's best to listen to your boss, Beaudry."

I got up and hugged Nico.

My boss said, "Can we get back to work now?"

\# \# \#

Following is an excerpt
from another exciting
Lieutenant Beaudry adventure.

BANK SHOT

PREFACE
June 1986

The dirty dishes were piled high and unstable in the sink. A squadron of fruit flies circled the open jam jar on the counter. The smell of burnt toast had faded, but the savagery of this morning's confrontation still hung heavy in the kitchen.

Ray slapped the Formica tabletop; the shock tipped an empty Labatt's bottle to the floor.

"Your old man is nuttier than a squirrel turd. When he came at me with his whip cane, he had murder in his eye."

As graceful as a cambré ballet move, Andy stretched sideways and scooped the rolling beer bottle back to the tabletop.

"He's half your size. You didn't have to choke him."

"I just knocked him out long enough to tie him up in the barn. Let him stay there till he cools down."

"Dad's a violent man. He's always detested me. I wasn't the tough boy he wanted. He knows how to use that cane. When I was thirteen, he caught me playing with my weenie in the barn. He hurt me real bad."

"I won't let him touch you, don't you worry your

pretty blond head."

"I could never do anything right. He blames me for whatever goes wrong; the failure of the farm, the drought of two summers ago, anything, it's always my fault."

"He's a nut case. Two years ago, I was saving you from a gang rape in the showers of cellblock C. You had nothing to do with the drought, your mom dying in childbirth or your crazy dad losing the election for local mayor."

"He turned me in for the hit-and-run without blinking an eye." Andy said. "I was so drunk I didn't even know I'd stuck the girl that night until I saw the blood on the grill of the caddy the next day."

Ray leaned forward and clasped Andy's delicate hand in a solid grip.

"Shit happens. We deal with it. We have money from the bank job. I have friends that will get us out west, then to California. We'll ditch this hick town and start a new life together."

"I'm scared, really scared." Andy tucked his chin into his chest and raised his shoulders as if imitating a frightened turtle. "I think you killed the lady."

"Her fault. When I told her to get on the floor, she slapped me in the face, my gun went off."

"There was a lot of blood; it was the same when Gill got shivved in the neck the day before his parole. He died right there in the yard."

At the creak of the floorboards, they both turned

toward the hallway entrance where the old man stood with the rifle aimed at his son's head.

There was no anger in the act, and no remorse. Putting down animals that were too sick to cure, was something that had to be done while he still had the strength. The bodies, as well as the Marlin bear gun went into the dried- up well on the east side of the barn. The old man ploughed over the site and relocated the manure pile over the makeshift grave. He survived another eight months until the metastasized lung cancer finally killed him.

To this day, the bank robbery and the murder of Eva Beaudry remain unsolved.

ONE

I had just reached my desk, when my phone rang. I moved a file or two to free the receiver. The small screen announced Capt. Jean O'Neil the extension number for my boss. I felt like letting it go to voicemail, but that would only delay the inevitable. I picked up the receiver and answered my usual, "Talk to me."

"You missed the morning meeting. Get to my office."

O'Neil hung up before I could explain about my need to wait for a delivery. It was going to be one of those Mondays. The meme of Linus tugging at his security blanket and an alligator pulling the other end came to mind as I quick marched to the Captain's office.

He had folders tiled across his desk, some opened, and some closed, as if he was sorting them by date or by importance.

As I plopped into his visitor chair, Jean said.

"Nice of you to finally drop in, Lieutenant Beaudry."

His little gray caterpillar mustache was downturned, his usual grumpy greeting for me.

"Did they give you a raise?"

He ignored my question, and read a hand-written comment from a yellow sticky-note pasted on the first page of a crime scene report.

"You replaced your green ratty old leather chair with a modern chrome and pleather high back," I said.

"I've got lumbar ache from this monstrosity and a pain in my butt from your last *fracas* in Chinatown," he retorted.

"I solved the case and apprehended the murderer without firing a shot." I put both my palms up as if waiting for a gift. "That must be worth something."

"A very expensive something, I just got the estimate for the restaurant damages," the Captain said.

"He refused to cooperate. He went Bruce Lee on me."

Jean sat in his new chair, "Apparently he was no match for your bulldozer moves. The hospital said that he may never get full use of his left wrist or elbow."

"The little skinny guy was incredibly fast," I said. "He got in some serious punches. It was like fighting a half a dozen snakes all at the same time. I was tired of being slapped around. I'm still black and blue from a week ago."

"My heart bleeds for you, but not as much as he did when you put him through the decorated plate glass. That, by the way, adds fifty- three hundred to the overall damages."

"Apparently, the dragon etching was from a famous oriental artist," I said. "I heard it several times from the owner. I didn't know they had so many curses and swear words in Cantonese."

"The doctor put you back on active duty. I expect you to report in on time."

Jean gave me *the speak-to-the-hand* signal. I never got the chance to explain about the new appliances delivery.

"This morning's meeting was a review of the Martel murder," Jean said."You're assigned to the team as CC's partner."

"What happened to Ron?"

"If you showed up at the office once in a while, you'd know his wife has cancer. He's on leave during her chemo."

"Ah, rats, sorry to hear that."

O'Neil's mustache straightened, the only sign of an attempted smile on his normally stern face.

"You okay working with CC?"

CC was Carol Curran– one of the three female detectives on the Major Crimes Homicide squad, and an old office flirtation of mine.

"I'm fine working with Carol, she's a smart cookie. But I'm not sure that your niece will be much pleased."

Both corners of his mustache curled down.

"Yeah, Pat told me that you're moving in with her."

"We've bought a house together, we're moving in with each other."

"Never mind the semantics. If she ever comes bawling to me because of you, my threat to core you like an apple still stands."

"It'll never happen. She's the apple of my eye and the core of my heart," I said.

The Captain pointed to the door. The man has no sense of *repartee* or humor.

I left his lair and took the stairs headed to Carol's cubicle on the next floor, a new murder case, and, probable troubles with my hot-tempered redheaded significant other, who knew of my history with Carol.

TWO

Carol was probably on the second morning coffee of her six- or- seven a day habit. According to her, caffeine kept her wired, vigilant and contributed to keeping her slim, tight figure. To the latter, I could testify in the affirmative.

As I approached, her pale blue eyes peeked at me from over the rim of her oversized gold mug. "Here comes my big muscled hero to save me from the dragon of tedium."

I was used to comments about my size. Descendant from a family of sturdy farmers and years of weight training gave me the appearance of a young Schwarzenegger. Wide shouldered and five-nine in height, I presented a solid square image. It earned me the nickname "Fridge."

I pulled an office chair from the desk next to Carol's and moved it close enough to get a whiff of her perfume.

It brought back a fond memory of my waking to an empty bed, but with her scent of musk and jasmine still lingering on my pillow.

She wore an above-the-knee pencil skirt, of medium blue, the color of a Montreal bus driver uniform. Her off-white, well-filled blouse and frilly V-neck allowed a peek at some cleavage. She looked at me with a mischievous grin on her kisser.

"You want some coffee or are you interested in something else?"

I changed the direction of my gaze.

"No I'm fine for coffee. You've changed your hair color. I like the lighter streaks and the shorter pixy cut, it makes you look even sassier."

"Your compliments are superfluous and gratuitous; I'm already wearing a black lacy thong in your honor."

"Your usual flirty self I see, but what's with the four- dollar words? You reading a thesaurus instead of the murder book?"

"You're the one always quoting poets and famous writers. I'm stepping up my game."

"Confucius said, *'Without knowing the force of words, it is impossible to know more.'* In any case, your eyes always say more than your tongue," I said.

Carol winked at me, put aside a small stand-up calendar of topless firefighters, and pulled out a slim file from the color- coded stack on her desk.

She dropped it on my lap.

"We better get to work before I slide off of my seat," she said.

It was getting hot in her office. I didn't respond to her last comment. I skimmed the documents for a minute or so, and then handed her back the file. She put it back on her stack and replaced the sexy firemen calendar on top.

"The Captain doesn't tolerate *any* girlie pics in the shop. What's with the firemen poses?"

"You're the famous detective, you figure it out."

"I'm going to need all of my skills on your case, there's not much to read in this file. Can you give me your version of the story?"

"It *looks* like a professional hit. The VIC drove into his garage, the perp was waiting inside, hidden. The first shot hit Martel in the jaw. The second and third entered just above the ear. The perp left, closing the garage door behind him. The wife was in the bedroom and didn't hear anything. Close neighbors heard, and saw nothing. End of story."

"You said -'*looks like*.' Why?"

"Because, there seems to be no *why*. Martel's not in the rackets. No criminal record. Not even a traffic ticket. He's appreciated and respected by neighbors and friends. So far he's a stand-up guy."

"You've checked out the business angle?"

"Dennis Martel owns a successful cell phone

franchise. You don't whack someone for a dropped call."

"Nothing from his past?"

"We've been on this for the last ten days. The guy is clean. The boss said we need a new pair of eyes on this." Carol's voice dropped to a sad hushed tone. "Twenty-one months ago, Martel married his high school sweetheart. Their first baby is due at the end of the month."

"Who found him?"

"The wife."

"Ouch. How is she?"

"Under a doctor's care. She's a total wreck. I couldn't get a word out of her. She's gone catatonic."

"This is turning into a real sad story," I said. "The news vultures are going to milk this for weeks."

Carol nodded.

"An unexplained assassination. The press are already speculating a deranged killer is on the loose. Pressure from the brass is building up fast on the case."

"Who's got forensics on this?"

"The nerd. Dobson."

"He may look like a nerd with his oversized glasses, but don't underestimate him. The kid is brilliant."

Carol shrugged.

"He found a partial palm print on the car roof,

but it doesn't match anything we have on record.

The ballistics report is on the last page in the file."

"Yup, I caught his comment, twenty-two caliber bullets and low penetration. A strong indication of sub-sonic loads or a suppressor."

"A professional hit, but zero motive," Carol said. "Perhaps, mistaken identity?"

With her remark, she made a cute wide-eyed funny face, her mouth in an exaggerated pout. It brought my attention to her very pink lips. Carol always managed to exude an air of seduction, seemingly without really trying. I was madly in love with Patricia, my more-than- significant- other, but Carol wasn't Lassie. I hadn't gone blind to her feminine attributes and charms.

I brought my thoughts from down south back to business.

"I highly doubt that," I said. "The killer was waiting in ambush. He had cased the place before. He knew there was no alarm on the garage, knew how to get in, and where to hide. It's not the M.O. of a street punk who would hit the wrong victim. This was carefully planned."

Carol stood up, and from her office coat rack unhooked a black belted raincoat patterned with large white polka dots.

"I'm for starting back at square one," she said,

we must have missed something. Let's head over to the crime scene."

"My Jeep is in the shop, trading the winter tires for summer rubber. You okay to drive?"

"Better me than you," she said. "Your reputation for wrecking cars and trucks precedes you."

"I barely dented the snow plow. In the storm, it was the only thing available to commandeer."

Carol gave me her full- wattage smile then turned on a heel. Admiring the rear view, I followed her to the outside parking lot.

Bank Shot is available in a paperback book or as an e-book from Amazon or from www.kentwiter.com.
The paperback is available to major bookstores from Ingram Distribution.

MICHAEL KENT is a retired international management and coaching consultant. Contrary to his technical writing, his fiction always has tinge of humor and a special twist to the tale.

A native of Montreal, he is bilingual, normally in the same sentence. Years as a private pilot, avid reading and extensive traveling, have generated a storehouse of plots and stories to be shared with the world.

http://www.kentwriter.com/

The Lieutenant Beaudry series:

Blood tail
Folded dreams
Twice dead
Tainted Evidence
Bank Shot
Dead of Winter
Unlucky Number

Michael Kent

Excerpt Bank Shot

Michael Kent